A DEATH OF INNOCENCE

A DEATH OF INNOCENCE

DAVID PENNY

RIVERTREE PRINT

MAY 1453: LEMSTER, THE ENGLISH MARCHES

When thirteen-year-old Thomas Berrington is attacked by a group of boys on his way home, he believes it is just another beating he must take—until one of the boys is found dead, and Thomas is accused of the murder.

Fighting to save his reputation and his life, Thomas is distracted by his feelings toward a girl his father would disapprove of: the pretty and resourceful Bel Brickenden. Together they uncover a web of deceit and lies to reveal the sad truth behind the murder. Meanwhile, another kind of death has come to Lemster—one that cannot be solved by reason alone.

A Death of Innocence is the first of three prequels relating the story of how Thomas Berrington comes to leave England and begin his travels to Moorish al-Andalus.

CHAPTER ONE

When Thomas Berrington saw the three boys standing on a makeshift bridge across the River Lugge, he knew there was going to be trouble. He had no idea how long they had been waiting there, or even if they were waiting for him, but he suspected they were. And that might prove a problem. Perhaps, he thought, I should have risked the travellers' camp after all.

He knew each of the boys, knew their names and their families, but that knowledge only added to his unease. Two of them carried sticks, elm by the look, though they were still too distant to be sure. The third, Symon Dawbney, no doubt believed he needed no stick, which might well be true. At fifteen, almost two years Thomas's senior, he was tall and wide across the shoulders. The Dawbneys paid rent to Thomas's father, Squire John Berrington, as did the Wodalls, but that wouldn't stop Symon giving him a beating if he could, nor Thomas's father John Berrington saying he no doubt deserved it.

Concealed by a hawthorn coming into full leaf, Thomas studied them. That they were waiting for him was beyond doubt, he decided. He had seen Walter Gifforde and Raulf Wodall in Lemster's town square after the morning sale had been concluded. They had taunted him, Raulf throwing stones, which had missed. They had no doubt gone in search of Symon, wanting his strength, and Symon would have been more than happy to join them. Thomas might have wondered why they hated him so much, but he knew it wasn't only him. They were of an age when boys became men, and the process burned through them with a confused fire quenched only by violence. One day they might go too far, kill someone and hang for it.

Not today, he hoped.

Thomas considered his options. It was a quarter mile back to the town bridge over the Lugge, another mile from there along the roadway to home. And there were the travellers who had set up camp in the field beyond the bridge, come for the Spring Fair. Tough men and even tougher women. Thomas would prefer not to pass that way if he didn't have to.

He glanced at the sky. There were several hours of daylight left, but he was tired, and some determination in him didn't want to see the three of them win this test of wills. Maybe he too was coming into manhood, despite the lack of hair around his cock, because he felt a cold anger grow inside him. This was *his* way home, and they had come deliberately to confront him. Would they be satisfied to give him a black eye, a bruise on his temple—or did they want more? If so, how much more? Thomas had heard tales about Symon Dawbney, no doubt some of them started by Symon himself. One even claimed he had killed a man. Not a boy, but a full-grown man. Self-defence, it was said, as they were attacked by bandits as he rode with his father from Ludlow one evening. But there were tales aplenty and Thomas

2

believed only what he could see. And what he could see was the three of them blocking his way home.

He wasn't even aware he had made a decision until he stepped from behind the hawthorn and walked toward the crossing. The felled oak spanned the river, deep here and slow moving. This field was farmed by the Dawbneys', though it was Thomas's father who held the deeds. Sheep grazed in one corner, four cattle beside them. The hedges were high. They needed cutting back because they were thinning at the base, but Thomas knew it was unlikely to be done. Sixty of their own sheep had been sold in Lemster today. Fine lambs, born that Spring and now grown fat on rich river grassland. It was the first Friday of the month, the market had been busy with their stink and sound, traders coming from as far away as Gloucester and Shrewsbury. As he walked, Thomas patted the purse at his waist to make sure the note of promise still lay safe in its oilskin wrap. Sixty sheep at a shilling a head. Good money, some of which his father was drinking and whoring away at the appropriately named Star Inn, for that is what he would no doubt be seeing before the night was over. What Thomas might be seeing too, if those yew sticks landed a blow.

He walked on, back straight, head held high, refusing to show any fear. Strangely, it worked, bringing confidence. He might be able to win the fight—and fight it would be, he was sure of that—but then again, he might not. Losing fights wasn't so bad. He'd lost many in the past, although fewer of late. No, losing was tolerable, and there would be no tales told, not by him.

The boys stood in a line where thick branches jutted from the wide trunk of the oak. Thomas had no idea how long it had lain there—ever since he had been old enough to

3

walk this way, and even then it had been weathered and worn smooth by the crossing of many feet.

"Hey, look, it's Tommy tit-mouse." Symon might be big, but he was not renowned for his intelligence or wit.

Thomas nodded, kept walking until he reached the riverbank, and then stopped. The water ran deep and smooth, threads of green weed fluttering in the current. He had fished here often, catching stupid chub and dace, but also wily, sweet-fleshed trout. Salmon passed this way in the Autumn, but a net was needed for those.

"Where you going, Tommy?" said Symon, and Walter Gifforde sniggered. So—fight it was to be.

"You got any coin?" said Raulf. He was the clever one, but sly, always looking for an advantage. Always willing to do someone down if it might bring him benefit, however small.

"Got no silver," Thomas said. He turned his pockets out to prove it.

"You sold three score sheep to Pa today," said Raulf. "I saw it. At a shilling a head. That's three pounds in anyone's money."

"Nobody pays in coin," Thomas said. "Even someone as stupid as you ought to know that." He wanted them angry. Angry boys acted too fast, acted without thinking. "Besides, I wager stealing three pounds might be a hanging offence."

"Only if someone tells," said Symon.

A serious fight, then. Possibly more than Thomas had considered. And it was true, three pounds was a goodly sum, which is why its theft would warrant the rope. It also warranted a risk.

"Who saw you on your way here?" Thomas asked, forcing his limbs to loosen. They wanted to draw tight, but he'd been in enough fights to know that would be a mistake.

"Nobody saw us," Raulf said. "We didn't let them."

"Somebody always sees something," Thomas said.

He glanced at Walter, who had said little so far. Thomas believed Walter the most afraid, the least committed to what was coming. He decided he would hit him first, send him into the river, and then it would be two against one. He tried to remember if Walter could swim, but the memory wouldn't come to him. No matter. The water shallowed over a bank of stones a hundred paces downstream where, before the oak fell, people would have forded the river.

"If you move aside I'll pass on by and there'll be no trouble," Thomas said.

Raulf Wodall laughed, an unpleasant sound. The laugh revealed gaps in his teeth, those that remained stained brown. Perhaps I can knock another one loose, Thomas thought, and before they were ready, he launched himself onto the trunk and at them.

As he expected, Walter Gifforde jerked back. Too hard, which meant Thomas didn't have the chance to grab his yew stick before he tipped backward into the water. Walter screamed, voice high like a girl, arms and legs thrashing. He sank beneath the surface, appeared five paces further downstream, the current here as strong as it was invisible.

"You pushed him," said Symon Dawbney. He was slow to move, and it was Raulf Wodall who struck first, his stick whistling through the air to crack against Thomas's arm. If he had not raised it fast, the blow would have landed on his head and sent him into the river after Walter.

At last Symon started forward, treading carefully, his balance not as good as Thomas's or Raulf's. To Thomas, the trunk was as good as a roadway. He felt secure, placed. When Symon swung a haymaker blow at him, Thomas simply stepped back and ducked. As soon as the blow swung above his head, he darted forward and kicked out, catching Symon on the thigh. The big lad went down on one knee, clutching his leg. Thomas moved forward again, thinking he could tip Symon in after Walter. He knew if he did, Raulf would turn and run. Sly he might be, but that only made him want to save his own skin the more. Except, as he moved, picturing the action in his head, Raulf's stick came from nowhere and cracked hard against the back of his skull.

Thomas went to his knees, hands on the smooth trunk.

"Hold on while I search him." It was Raulf, still convinced there was money somewhere.

"You heard what he said. If we steal his coin it's a whipping at least, a rope at worst." Still, Symon wrapped his arms around Thomas, preventing him from rising. Raulf came close, his hands patting pockets, searching inside Thomas's shirt, coming close to where the purse lay against his skin. It would do him no good if he did find it. The note was made out to John Berrington, but Raulf might take it and destroy it out of spite, stealing the money from them even if it didn't end up in his own pocket.

As Raulf came closer, confident now, Thomas reared up and his head cracked into Raulf's chin. He staggered back, hands to his mouth, blood dripping between his fingers. Thomas smiled. He'd loosened a tooth, then. Good.

Symon heaved, lifting Thomas off his feet. Thomas's legs flailed, but although he connected once or twice, Symon was ready for him.

"Hold him," Raulf said, gathering himself. He came in hard and fast, fists flailing, and Thomas had no choice but to take them. He felt his own lip split, one eye close up. Then he twisted as he felt Symon's hold slacken for a brief moment and he kicked out again, catching Raulf between the legs. The boy sighed and went to his knees, clutching himself. Then Symon turned and threw Thomas into the river.

He kicked underwater, swimming as far as he could on the single breath he had managed to draw before the river took him. When he surfaced, he glanced back. Symon was trying to help Raulf to his feet, but the younger boy was shaking his head. Thomas grinned and turned over, kicking his legs to bring him more swiftly to the shingle.

When he reached it, Walter Gifforde lay half on the bank, his legs still in the water.

"You could have drowned me," he said. "Drowned me, Tom!"

"Raulf had worse planned for me than a drowning, didn't he?" Thomas had nothing against Walter except the company he kept.

Walter looked away, unwilling to meet Thomas's stare.

Thomas waded across the shingle. He patted Walter on the head as he passed and the boy flinched. He strode out across the field. When he glanced back, Symon was still trying to help Raulf walk. Thomas grinned, hoping he might have done some permanent damage. But when he slid his hand beneath his soaked shirt and drew out the promissory note, his grin melted away. He pressed the oiled cloth between his palms, wincing as water dripped from it, wincing even more when he saw the stain of ink on his fingers.

CHAPTER TWO

"I can't do anything with this," said Thomas's mother, Catherine. Catherine Watkins as was, before she had agreed to marry John Berrington. He was a catch, it was claimed, but if so, a catch with barbs, and fists too keen to search out an easy target.

The promissory note sat on the kitchen table, little more than damp now. His mother had brought a lamp close, its wavering light showing where the ink had run.

"Do you remember what it said?" she asked.

"You can see what it says." Thomas pointed, noticing his fingers were still stained, scarce believing the ink could have run so much from the vellum, but stayed so stubborn on his skin. "It says, 'I, Peter Markel, on behalf of Arthur Wodall who promises to pay John Berrington the sum of sixty shillings on or before Lammas day in the year of Our Lord 1452, witness this note of promise on the1st day of May. Signed Peter Markel as Agent to John Talbot, Earl of Shrewsbury.'"

"It says all that?" His mother leaned closer, screwing her eyes up. "John Talbot was in town today?"

"No, only his agent, for the May Fair. And perhaps I only recall what it did say," Thomas said. "But I'm sure I can read some of the pieces, here, and here."

"Did Arthur Wodall sign it?"

Thomas shook his head. "Made his cross. More important is Peter Markel did." His face fell. "And used the Talbot stamp on it too. Down here." He picked at a remnant of wax.

His mother looked up. "What will your father do?"

"You know what he'll do, Ma—he'll beat me."

She nodded. "No doubt you deserve a beating for this, Thomas. What were you thinking of?"

"I was thinking of getting home," he said. "And it was not me did this. I told you, this is the fault of those boys. Each of them. Though Walter less than the others, I suppose."

"Symon Dawbney would not do this," said his mother. "His family pays rent to us each quarter day. His father is a good man."

His father is a bully and an idiot, Thomas thought, but didn't say so. Instead he leaned closer, careful not to cast a shadow on the document. He peered at it, trying to work out if what he saw was truly writing, or no more than his mind casting shapes.

"Sixty shillings," he said when he sat back. His arm ached from where Raulf Wodall's stick had caught him. There would be a fine bruise growing, but he wouldn't mention that to his mother. He would hide his arm until the bruise faded. She worried enough about him already.

"We can't afford to lose sixty shillings." Her voice was barely audible, and Thomas knew her words were true. John Berrington might own much land, might be lauded as squire to the Earl of Shrewsbury, but sixty shillings was a small fortune and the coming winter would be harder for its loss.

9

Thomas glanced at the small window. Mottled glass dimmed the day outside to a grey-green tint, almost the same colour he had seen beneath the Lugge's surface. At least they had windows with glass in them, which was more than most in town could boast of.

"I might be able to do something."

His mother glanced up from where she had been studying the vellum, as if the power of her stare would be enough to burn the letters back into existence.

"There's nothing there, Thomas."

"I know what it said." He rose, folded the vellum carefully and tucked it back into the leather purse, which had almost dried. "Don't say anything to Pa when he comes in. I'll see what I can do come morning."

"What do you intend to do? You're not to do anything to those boys, Thomas." His mother stood, but made no move toward him. "What if your father asks about the note when he comes in?"

"You know he won't be coming home any time soon." There was no need to state the reason. Catherine Berrington was an intelligent woman. Too intelligent for the likes of her husband, intelligent enough to know she needed a protector. John Berrington was a boor of a man, a bully who thought only of his own needs, but he had land and some small status in a small town. It would prove enough, until it was no longer.

* * *

As Thomas made his way back across early morning fields toward Lemster, the grass half-hidden beneath a layer of drifting mist, he veered north to avoid the crossing he had been tossed from the evening before. He didn't expect the boys would have come to wait for him again, but preferred to avoid the risk. He would watch out for them when he entered town, sure if they caught sight of him, a beating was likely. The Priory he made for was south of Bridge Street, and he knew alleys that would allow him to avoid any other early risers.

The sun had barely risen, the light was cold and long shadows cast across the fields from hedgerows. A flock of crows crossed the sky, their raucous cries filling the air as they headed to their roosts. Cattle and sheep grazed the fields. Those to the north belonged to Thomas's father, those to the south were Arthur Wodall's, marked with green dye in case any beasts wandered. The hedges were markers, not intended to keep a determined animal captive.

At the old stone bridge on the Ludlow Road, Thomas caught sight of Symon Dawbney sitting on a wall where the Kenwater ran beneath. He was whittling at a stick, which meant he had a knife.

Thomas turned aside from the way he wanted to go and followed the far side of a scruffy hawthorn hedge until he was well past Symon. This way took him through the fields the travellers had been camped at for the May Fair, but he was glad to see most had packed up and moved on to the next gathering. Thomas had nothing against them, but that didn't mean he trusted them. He rejoined the road close to where an old woman leaned over with a hacking cough. He made sure to avoid her. People said the travellers brought disease and there had been rumours of people falling ill with the blue sickness in Oxford and Gloucester. Thomas was relieved when he could finally push through a thin hedge to reach Broad Street.

The Priory grounds had no clear defining border. Thomas passed a stew pond where fat carp rolled lazily to the surface, others making the cloudy water shimmer as they moved beneath. Small vegetable plots appeared, then a low stone wall. Beyond, the Priory grew ever more impressive, as it was meant to.

Thomas headed toward the right-hand corner, his destination in mind. As he passed the side of the building, he heard the brothers chanting their prayers. He stopped to listen, his skin tightening at the sound. He attended church every Sunday with his family, but the prayers he recited there never had the same effect they did here. With over a hundred voices rising together, he understood why men felt closer to God. He had considered taking the cloth, but knew he lacked a pure enough heart. His body was changing, and with it his emotions. He looked at girls differently now. And girls looked at him differently too.

Thomas glanced toward the town, wondering if he should check on his father, who had not returned home. The last Thomas had seen of John Berrington, he had been clutching a flagon of ale. He had drunk enough to appear almost in a good mood.

"How old are you now, Tom?" he had asked.

"You know how old, Father." He hated being called Tom. His mother always called him Thomas, but however hard he tried, few others did.

"Go on, remind me."

"Thirteen years, Father."

John Berrington nodded at a pretty young woman who was sitting nearby. "Do you like Jilly here? She'll take you upstairs for a farthing and make a real man of you, won't you, Jilly?"

"Not for a farthing."

"A penny then."

"Aye, he can come upstairs with me for a penny. He's a pretty enough boy, ain't he?"

"Too skinny, though," said John Berrington. "And he

reads books. But he can pull a longbow well, so there's hope for him yet. What do you think, Tom? Have you got a penny? Do you want to become a man?"

That had been when Thomas walked out of the inn. Not that he didn't want to become a man, but he knew how many others had been with Jilly over the years and didn't want to start his education with a dose of the pox. Besides, he hadn't got a penny.

Thomas grew aware the chanting had come to an end and the brothers were making their way out of the Priory. This was their time for work, prayers complete until noon. Some returned to their plots, others walked in groups, talking. Thomas saw Brother Bernard in conversation and waited until he separated from his companions and came toward him, which meant he was going to the sacristy.

"You look like you've been in a fight, Tom," Brother Bernard said. The brother's glance took him in from head to toe. "And you look like you've slept in those clothes."

"I fell in the river," Thomas said.

"Unfortunate. And the fight?"

Thomas shrugged. There were always fights, and he barely felt any discomfort anymore. "It was nothing. Raulf Wodall caught me with a stick is all. An elm stick."

"A good wood for a stick," said Brother Bernard. "You've got a fine bruise coming. What was the fight over?"

"I already said, it was no fight." Thomas reached into his purse. "This got wet."

Brother Bernard stared at the folded vellum. "What is it?"

"A note of promise for sixty shillings."

"Made out to whom?" They were walking side by side toward the sacristy, which was set hard against the back wall of the Priory.

"Father."

"Ah. I take it this note of promise is not in pristine condition?"

"It got wet," Thomas said. "I thought you could, I don't know, fix it?"

"Fix it?" said Brother Bernard.

"Or something."

Brother Bernard pushed open the heavy oak door to the sacristy and led the way inside. This was his domain, but one familiar to Thomas too. His father was right, he did possess a love of books, but it was nothing he was ashamed of. Maps too. And tales of distant lands and strange places. Places such as those Brother Bernard had seen and, when the mood was on him, he talked of. He also taught Thomas how to read and write better than he already could. He was even teaching him a little French and a few words of Spanish, which he had acquired before taking the cloth. Such tales. Such exotic places and names. Calais. Seville. Cordoba. Carcassonne. The words almost as sweet on Thomas's tongue as a knob of honey.

"Give it to me." Brother Bernard held out his hand and Thomas handed the note across. Sunlight fell through the windows as Brother Bernard unfolded the note and laid it on a table where the best of that light lay. He drew up a stool and nodded for Thomas to do the same.

Brother Bernard pulled out a drawer and rummaged within, drew out a glass and held it over the parchment so it appeared magnified.

"What did it say?" he asked.

"The usual. I Peter Markel, Agent to—well, all the usual stuff—promise to pay John Berrington the sum of sixty shillings in exchange for three score head of Ryland sheep, to be paid in full on or before Lammas day on production of this note of promise. Signed by Peter Markel."

"You have a good memory."

"Someone in our family needs one."

Brother Bernard tapped Thomas on top of the head. "Honour thy mother and thy father."

"Yes, Brother," Thomas said. "I'll try."

Brother Bernard stood and wandered off, lifting papers and opening drawers until he found what he was looking for. He returned with a box, the lid made of a single sheet of fine glass. He went back and brought lamps, lit six and placed them inside the box and closed the lid. Thomas examined it to discover the lid was angled so the smoke of the lamps came out through an opening at the back.

When Brother Bernard laid the parchment on the glass, the light came from beneath the glass and made it semi-transparent. The writing was clearer, and Thomas believed he could almost read it.

Brother Bernard tapped the parchment. "The question I must ask now is whether restoring this note is ethical or not." He glanced at Thomas. "Tell me how you came to get it wet enough to wash the ink from it."

"I fell in the Lugge," Thomas said.

"I did not take you to be so clumsy, Tom. Tell me what really happened. Did it have something to do with a stick fashioned of elm, perhaps?"

Thomas said nothing.

"Was it another fight?" Brother Bernard knew all about the fights Thomas got into. He had stitched his brow after one when the wound was too deep to heal unaided.

Thomas still said nothing.

Brother Bernard straightened and pushed the parchment away. "Ah well, in that case I cannot judge, and if I cannot judge, I cannot help."

"There were boys on the old oak log across the river. They were waiting for me."

"And Raulf Wodall was one of them?"

"He was."

"Did he know of this note?"

Thomas thought back. Had Raulf been at the sale? He didn't recall seeing him, but before they fought on the river crossing, he'd said he knew about the note.

"He might have."

"Perhaps his father asked him to toss you in the river, knowing this would be spoiled and he would have no need to pay your father his sixty shillings."

"It's possible." Thomas knew Brother Bernard was building his own justification. "Except Raulf Wodall knows he can't beat me in a fight, fair or not."

"So he asked…" Brother Bernard tapped his fingers on the parchment, drawing it back into the middle of the glass lid. "Let me see, Walter Gifforde and, of course, Symon Dawbney. You've had run-ins with Symon before, haven't you?"

"Once or twice."

"And more, I don't doubt." He stared at the parchment, pursed his lips. "But still I would find it hard to undertake a task so close to forgery."

"Restoration, surely?" Thomas said.

Brother Bernard glanced at him. "In your mind, perhaps. My own is not so certain. But perhaps I could teach you the art of restoring a document. Would you be interested?"

Thomas nodded.

Brother Bernard peered once more at the parchment. "There isn't much left, is there?"

"I can almost see it as it was," Thomas said.

"Then you may be able to do something." He lifted the parchment and handed it to Thomas. "Take it outside and piss on it."

"What?"

"I didn't know you were hard of hearing. Take it outside and piss on it. If you can, that is. I don't know when last you passed water. If you have none, go ask one of the brothers. One of the older ones. They seem to need to go piss all the time. Your water will bring what ink is left to the surface."

Thomas looked at the parchment, looked at Brother Bernard to see if he was joking, as he sometimes did. He saw in this instance he wasn't.

"And when you piss on it, do so on the back, not the front. We don't want to wash any more away, do we?"

Thomas got up and went outside to find a quiet corner.

CHAPTER THREE

Thomas glanced at Brother Bernard. He was a tall man, broad across the shoulders, slim in the body. He had a scar above one eye, another on his arm. Thomas had asked about them and sometimes Brother Bernard weakened and told him stories of his time in Spain. But not today.

When Thomas examined the parchment, treated and dried now but still with a sharp smell rising from it, he did think the letters looked clearer.

"How does it work?" he asked.

"There is *amun* in your water. It strengthens the ink, particularly when you dry it close to a flame. I don't know why, only that it does. Can you read it now?"

Thomas peered at the letters. "I think so. When did you learn how to do that?"

"In Castile," said Brother Bernard. "From an old man, not a Spaniard, one of those Moorish men. He seemed to know more than was natural in a man, but most of what he taught me has proved useful, so perhaps he wasn't all bad."

"Did you fight him?"

Brother Bernard rose from his stool and stretched his back. "Why ever would I do that? He helped me, taught me much."

"But you fought in Spain, didn't you?"

"I did. And I learned one side is just as bad, and just as good, as any other. It is why I returned to England and took the cloth." Brother Bernard clipped Thomas around the ear, a soft slap to return his attention to the task at hand. "I will let you get on with your work."

"Aren't you going to help?"

"I told you, I don't approve of fabrication." Brother Bernard stared at Thomas a moment longer, then turned and left.

Thomas laid the parchment on the glass box again and picked up the circle of glass that made the letters clearer. There was ink and a pen on the table, which Brother Bernard had somehow managed to place there without taking part in the process of forgery. The ink was of fine quality, the same as used on the illustrated pages scattered about the sacristy. Possibly too fine a quality, and Thomas wondered if he needed to water it down, then decided against. He would try a little first and see how it looked.

He dipped the pen, wiped most of the ink off, then leaned close, the stink of his own piss catching in his nose. He tilted his head, trying to judge where the first letter started, then began to write over the faint outline. At first his hand trembled and the letters looked wrong, but after a while he found the trembling slackened. He worked on as the light grew through the window. Somewhere a voice shouted, but he barely heard it. Other voices came from outside, but still he worked on.

When he finally straightened, his back protested and his

arm ached. He stood, twisting from side to side, then leaned over and studied the parchment, worried it looked too good.

The letters were crisp, neat and sharp.

Thomas wondered if the smell of piss would fade. It would do him no good if when the letter was handed over in demand of payment, it smelled like a dog had lifted its leg on it. Or perhaps not. Such things happened often enough in Lemster to draw little comment.

Arthur Wodall's signature was nothing more than his mark, but that was proper because the man could barely write. Even if he had learned how to sign a document, he didn't know how to read one, and neither could his son. In fact, Thomas didn't know anyone his age who could read. It wasn't a skill much respected in these parts. Strong shoulders, powerful arms, those gained respect. The ability to draw a meaning from scratchings on a page meant nothing, but looking around the sacristy, Thomas knew those scratchings might be the most powerful thing on God's earth. There were worlds and ideas captured between leather bindings here that opened his eyes to wonders he would never see. The words painted pictures in his mind, of far-off lands and far-off peoples, and he felt an ache of regret they were barred to him. His world was constrained and small, limited by the boundaries of his father's land, and the extent of how far a man could walk in a day and back. He had been as far as Hereford and Ludlow. Once on a dare he had walked into Wales, fearful the whole time some red-painted devil might leap out at him. But the journey had proven uneventful other than for an old woman he had encountered at his furthest distance, who had pointed a gnarled finger at him and spoken in words he couldn't understand. He'd turned and run, too afraid to look back, scared she would be astride a broomstick flying after him.

He wanted to leave the ink a while longer yet to make sure it was fully dry, so he wandered the shelves, pulling down documents at random. He could read a little of those written in Latin, for they formed the majority and were what Brother Bernard used to teach him. Others were signs, nothing more, scribblings without meaning. A few had illustrations, drawings and maps. Thomas studied these closely, drawn by the mystery they represented, but knowing that maps were as close as he would ever get to the wonders of the world.

He expected Brother Bernard to return, but when after an hour he had not, Thomas checked the letter one last time. He rubbed some sand across the surface to blur the letters, folded it into his leather purse and left. There was no need to lock the sacristy. The Abbey had no locks.

Thomas walked west toward the centre of town. The market square was quieter now and he made his way to The Star to see if his father was still there. If so it would be safer to wait and accompany him home. Safer both for Thomas and John Berrington, who would be well into his cups by now.

Thomas peered through the mottled glass windows, their thickness distorting the figures within into some demonic gathering. He looked over the denizens but couldn't see his father. Arthur Wodall was there with a girl on his knee. Sunk into a dark corner sat the other John Berrington, Thomas's elder brother. There was little affection between the two. John considered Thomas a weakling and a coward. Thomas considered his brother stupid and a bully. There was no sign of Raulf or the other boys. Not until Thomas turned from the window.

Symon Dawbney and Raulf Wodall stood no more than ten feet away. They must have crept up as Thomas was looking into the inn.

"Not had enough yet, Tommy?" Symon said.

"I'm not looking to fight you again," Thomas said.

Symon grinned. "You may not be, but we are. We got unfinished business. You need a lesson teaching."

Thomas laughed, hoping to taunt the boys into rash action. He was close enough to the inn for a fight to bring people out and break it up. "I don't think you've got much to teach me, 'less it's how to be stupid."

"You can't rile me," Symon said, but his face told a different story.

"Just the two of you, is it?"

Symon smiled, showing gaps in his teeth. One had been made by Thomas, a lucky punch a month before which had so far gone unpunished. It might be what this was all about, but none of the boys needed much excuse.

"We sent Walter home for his brothers soon as we saw you," said Raulf. "They've been drinking most of the day, so'll be good and ready for a fight by now."

"You think they'll bother with me?" But Thomas was worried now. Walter Gifforde was the youngest of the sons. There were three others, two of them seventeen or older, broad shouldered from work on the farm. The Giffordes were considered lucky. Most of their children had survived disease or accident to grow to adulthood. Thomas's father reckoned Hugh Gifforde had been too busy servicing the whores of Lemster, Hereford and Ludlow to seed more, and his wife too grateful to draw attention to herself.

"We'll see, won't we?" said Raulf.

"Or I could just punch you both senseless and walk home before they arrive," Thomas said.

"They know where to find you."

"Even the Giffordes aren't stupid enough to attack me in my own home. The Prior would have them arrested and flogged, at the least."

"Hugh Gifforde pays good money to the Priory," said Raulf.

"As does my father. Even better I'd vouch." The boys were talking too much, waiting for the others to arrive. Thomas knew now was the time to act. He tensed, ready to lunge at them, when Symon's attention shifted to someone behind him. Thomas spun around, expecting an attack. Instead his brother John stood outside the inn, pissing into the street. When Thomas looked back, Symon and Raulf had taken two steps backward.

"What's going on, Tom?" asked John. He glanced at the two boys, back to Thomas.

"Nothing," Thomas said. "We were talking is all. Symon reckons he paid a penny and ploughed Arabella Brickenden. I said he was talking out of his arse, as usual."

John Berrington laughed. "God, Tom, everybody's ploughed Bel's mother, but I didn't know she'd followed in the family business or I'd have tupped her myself. Young girls need a man to show them how to do it right, and Bel surely is a pretty thing to set eyes on." John glanced at Symon. "Mind, I do expect Symon is talking out of his arse, like you say." He turned, re-tying his trousers.

"Is Pa inside?" Thomas asked fast before his brother left.

"He's talking with Peter Markel. Some kind of town business."

"It's getting time we went home," Thomas said.

John stopped and turned back, his head cocked to one side. "Are you mad, Tom? You can go if you want, but there are girls upstairs who'll do you for a penny, a nice young lad like you. They'd call it an investment." John laughed, turning away, leaving Thomas no choice but to fight.

CHAPTER FOUR

Thomas launched himself at Symon first because he was the bigger. Caught him hard on the side of the face, with luck loosening another tooth. Raulf punched Thomas in the back, but the blow carried no weight. Thomas hit Symon a second time until he went to one knee, then turned back to Raulf.

His brother had stopped outside the tavern door, watching the fight with a smile on his face.

"Do you want to come and help me out?" Thomas asked.

John shook his head. "Why would I want to do that? Besides, you're doing well enough on your own. You fight better than I reckoned you would."

Thomas whipped a fast punch to Raulf's chin, knocking him onto his back. "They sent Walter Gifforde to fetch his brothers. They'll be on their way back here by now."

John leaned against the wall and crossed his ankles. "That might prove more entertaining. Any idea when they're arriving?"

"I'll leave you to find out." Thomas turned away, starting

across the square. He'd only crossed half the distance when a hand caught his shoulder and spun him around. He raised his fists, ready to fight as long as he could, but instead of a Gifforde, it was his brother John who stood there.

"Berringtons don't run from a fight, Tom, you know that."

"Four against one?" Thomas said. "Six if either of those fools can stand." He shook his head. "No, I don't think so." He tried to pull away, but John had him caught firm, his fingers twisted into his shirt.

"If they look like they're going to kill you, I'll step in and help out, how does that sound?"

"Not so good. How close to death do you want me to get before you help?"

"A boy needs a few beatings to toughen him up. I took plenty but nobody tries coming at me anymore. It'll do you good, Tom."

Thomas rolled his shoulder in an attempt to loosen John's grip, but there wasn't enough give. The tavern door opened, light spilling out, and Sir John Berrington stepped out. He looked around and saw his two sons standing together.

"Hey, John, Jilly was asking where you'd got to." He glanced at Thomas. "Do you want a go with her after John's finished?" He laughed, making his opinion of Thomas's ability with women clear.

John released his grip and turned away. "Stay and take your punishment, Tom. You'll be the better for it."

Thomas had no intention of waiting. He backed away, turned. Which is when the Giffordes appeared from Corn Street, four of them spreading out as they entered the square. Hugh Gifforde, head of the family, came in the lead, always ready for a fight. Thomas turned again. He might be ready to flee, but he knew he couldn't be seen to run. He saw his father still outside the tavern, talking with John. With a slap on the back, the elder son disappeared inside. John Berrington senior turned his attention to his younger son, a spark in his eyes and a grin on his face.

"What's this about, then?"

"He pushed our Walter into the Lugge," said Hugh Gifforde. "Could have killed him. Left him for dead, anyways."

"Boys' pranks," John Berrington said. "As I recall, me and you had more than a few run-ins in our time, didn't we?"

"And took our punishment when we were in the wrong," said Hugh Gifforde. "Like your boy is going to take his punishment now."

John Berrington pushed himself away from the tavern wall and strode into the square, managing almost a straight line. Drink and pride, Thomas thought, made a dangerous mix.

Symon Dawbney was on his feet again, pulling at Raulf Wodall.

"What punishment do you have in mind?" John Berrington asked. He drew himself to his full height, which was impressive. He was a strong man, a hard man. He had fought alongside John Talbot, the Earl of Shrewsbury, in many a battle and always emerged if not unscathed, then alive.

"I was thinking perhaps a dunking in the Kenwater. Hold him under for a while, give him a taste of how it feels to drown."

John Berrington shook his head. "Sounds dangerous to me. Who'd be doing the holding under? You? Your boys?

One of these two?" He cast a disdainful look in Symon and Raulf's direction.

"This isn't your fight, John," said Hugh Gifforde. "Let Tom here take his punishment and we can all go home to our beds. Or back inside for second helpings, if you like."

"I don't like the idea of any drowning," said John Berrington. He glanced toward Thomas. "But if what I hear is right then a punishing is due. How about it, Tom? Did you try to drown young Walter here?"

"He slipped," Thomas said.

"Pushed," shouted Walter.

"Pushed me too," said Raulf Wodall. "And near enough knocked Symon out."

"Did not," said Symon, needing to show he was no easy target.

"How about they settle it among themselves? One on each side, last man standing." It was the kind of justice John Berrington favoured, but it didn't seem to be to Hugh Gifforde's liking.

"I hear your boy's good with his fists. Fast too."

"That's news to me," said John Berrington.

"One on one don't seem fair. I think it should be the three of them against Tom."

"Three on one? You think that's just, do you?"

"I can take them," Thomas said. "It's all right, Pa, I can take them all, easy."

John Berrington laughed. "Well, I'm seeing a whole new side of you tonight." He shook his head. "I'm wondering if maybe I've had too much to drink and this is all a dream."

"Three on one," said Hugh Gifforde, staring at Thomas. "You'll go three on one, Tom?"

Thomas nodded. He shook his arms to loosen the muscles, snapping the fear out through his fingertips.

Hugh Gifforde grinned. "Three on one it is, then." He looked around. "You ready, boys?"

Symon, Raulf and Walter nodded, but it was the other three sons who stepped forward. Adam, almost as tall as John Berrington, and if anything wider across the shoulders. Roger, slimmer but known to be sly. And Osmund, the second youngest, overweight, but the weight hid muscle.

"Them's not the three I meant," said John Berrington.

"P'raps not, but they's the three who are going to finish this thing." Hugh Gifforde nodded at his sons. He moved away to stand beside John Berrington. "Don't try to interfere, John, you know your boy needs to take his beating like a man."

"Aye, I expect he does." John Berrington looked at Thomas. "Are you all right with this, lad? I'll get you carried home after." Then, to the three youths, "Make sure you don't get too vexed and kill him."

And just like that, it was done, the die cast, the punishment made just.

The conversation had drawn others out from the tavern and, seeing a chance for entertainment, they spread out in a rough circle. Money started changing hands, but not for long. Nobody was willing to bet on Thomas, and there was little point else. A few small bets were made on who'd be the first of the three to knock Thomas over, most of the money going on Adam Gifforde. Which is why Thomas ran hard and kicked his knee out from under him.

Adam fell, screaming and clutching at his leg. The knee cap was dislodged, pushed out of position, and it would need one of the Monks to work it back into place, a process that would involve more pain than the blow itself had caused.

"You little bastard." Roger Gifforde reached behind and pulled out a knife that had been slipped into his belt.

"Drop it," said John Berrington. "This is a fair fight."

"Fair?" said Roger, spittle flying from his mouth. "Is it fair to break Adam's leg? Your boy needs teaching a lesson."

"Drop the knife," said Hugh Gifford, his voice soft but carrying a weight John Berrington's could not. His son cast a look at his father, another at Thomas, then reached around and pushed the knife into his belt again. It was the best they were going to get, so Thomas took four quick steps forward and punched Roger hard in the mouth. He felt teeth break and his own skin rupture. It was a foolish move made out of anger, which is why Thomas wasn't surprised when Osmund wrapped his arms around him from behind. He expected blows, but instead Osmund did no more than pin his arms down and hold him in place.

Roger Gifforde shook his head and spat blood. Anger made him shake, and Thomas knew he wanted to reach for the knife again, but there were too many witnesses and Roger didn't want to hang.

"Hold him still," he grunted. "And Walter, you come here too. It was you started this with your falling in the Lugge."

"I didn't fall, I was pushed." But Walter came to stand beside his brother. Symon Dawbney held back, but Raulf Wodall had no such reservations. His fist caught Thomas on the side of the head, snapping it around. Thomas kicked out, but the boy darted away. Then Symon took his turn, putting all his weight behind a blow to the belly. Then it was Roger's chance, not because he had any iron in this fire, but simply because he was bad to the core. He came slowly, shaking his arms. He slapped Thomas across the face, first one side then the other. He slapped harder, each blow an escalation until his fists closed and the blows began to bruise. Thomas felt other blows to his body, but Roger's strikes were taking their toll as they increased in ferocity and the world started to fade away. At least the pain went with it.

* * *

"God's teeth, Tom, but you're a mess, aren't you? I'll say this, though—you took your beating like a man."

Thomas opened one eye, the other refusing to obey him. His father leaned over him with a half-empty water bucket in one hand. He nodded, satisfied. "Aye, looks like you'll live."

"Why?" Thomas mumbled, the word jumbled against his tongue.

"Why did I let them?"

Thomas nodded, pain lancing down his neck.

"Because it was just." John Berrington offered a hand and Thomas took it, almost screaming as he was pulled to his feet. "Now come inside and take a drink for the pain."

"I don't want to come in." Thomas knew the Giffordes would be in there celebrating their victory, embellishing the tale until they became its heroes.

"Wait out here then," said John Berrington. "I need to finish some business with Peter Markel. He tells me there's been sickness in Gloucester and Oxford and we need to prepare in Lemster in case it comes here. He said it was a mistake to let those travellers pitch on the meadow at Eaton, but it's too late to change that now, I told him." He looked closer at Thomas and shook his head. "When we're finished, I'll put you on the back of the cart and get you home."

After his father was gone, Thomas put a hand against the wall, leaned over and vomited. He spat, wiped his mouth and washed it out with the remnant of water left in the bucket before wondering where it might have come from.

He mentally examined his body, noting where the worst blows had struck. He tried again to open his right eye, but with only limited success. He'd have to wait for morning. He ran his tongue along his teeth, surprised to find them all present. Then he moved away across the square, making for the tree across the Lugge which would take him home, hopefully this time without further incident.

Thomas stopped at the sound of voices as he approached the Priory, but it was only a couple doing what couples do, the woman's skirts raised almost to her chin while the man's backside showed pale in the moonlight. Thomas watched for a while, feeling a stirring inside his britches as he wondered what it would be like to lie with a woman. Perhaps he ought to return to the inn and beg a penny from his father, take it upstairs to Jilly, or better yet Joan Brickenden. Except he knew he would never do such a thing. Not yet, anyway, and certainly not in his current condition.

The man was making loud grunting noises now and Thomas moved on, not interested enough to stay for the inevitable conclusion. He'd been around stock long enough to know what was coming, except he knew people managed to make it last a little longer. Some of them, anyway.

He came out onto the water meadow of the Lugge, no more than damp underfoot in the Spring. The moon washed the pasture grey, trees standing stark on Eaton Hill. He thought he could make out a light where his own house stood and wondered if the mutton stew was still warm. His mother would no doubt have gone to bed by now.

Thomas rolled his shoulders, working his way around his body, testing the sore areas, knowing the bruises would fade in a week. There would need to be some retribution for the beating, but he couldn't work out what yet.

He had passed the big hawthorn where he had hidden to watch the boys when a noise sounded, the sharp snap of a branch. Thomas started to turn, raising his fists, but whoever was behind him moved faster. He didn't feel whatever struck his head, nor the ground when he tumbled to it.

CHAPTER FIVE

Whoever had done it, Thomas was sure they meant him dead. When he woke, he wondered why he wasn't. Awareness came slowly. He was uncomfortable, wet, and cold. Stone cold, shivering as soon as his body woke enough to respond. Thomas rolled over and immediately regretted it as his nose filled with water. He slumped to one side, forcing his eyes open. At least both of them seemed to be working now. It was still dark, but not as dark as it had been. Dawn was somewhere close, coming early at this time of year. He had been dragged from where he had been attacked and dumped in the Lugge. He'd been meant to drown, he was sure, but some fluke of good fortune had carried him against the branches of a fallen tree which lay half submerged. From above, it wouldn't be visible, not in the dark.

Thomas felt around with his hands, finding only slippery wood. He couldn't get a purchase and the steep mud bank lay eight feet away. Instead of exhausting himself further, he pushed away and let the current carry him. Thomas wasn't afraid of the water, knowing it would support him as long as he didn't panic. The river was deep here, slow running, and he floated beneath overhanging elm and willow until his toes touched the bottom. They found mud, and he waited a while longer, rewarded a little later by stones underneath. He stood, water draining from his clothes. He almost cried out at the realisation the note he had so carefully re-written would now be ruined again. He reached into his tunic, searching for the leather purse and failing to find it. So not just tipped in the river, but searched as well. But why? A note of promise was of no use to anyone other than the bearer. Not unless it was you who had made the promise, and then it would become null and save you sixty shillings. A substantial sum for John Berrington, a fortune for someone like Arthur Wodall, who wasn't known as an expert husbander of sheep. Plus he now had the sheep as well. So a saving of sixty shillings, and another sixty if he could sell them on. None of which did Thomas any good, not without the note or proof of who took it. Perhaps it wasn't Raulf or his father but one of the travellers, though most of them had left town now, taking their rumours of pestilence with them.

Thomas waded to the shore, pulled himself out and turned slowly to orient himself. He found Eaton Hill and started across the field. The effort warmed him, the climb through the woods warming him even more, so by the time the house came into view, his clothes were starting to steam a little. The light was stronger now, bringing colour to the grass, the trees and the barn. The house itself was never going to be anything other than black and white. Thomas wondered whether his father had made it back home, or if he still lay comatose in one of the upper rooms of The Star.

When Thomas pushed the door open, he found John Berrington asleep in the chair that only he was allowed to sit in, the one closest to the fire. His long legs were stretched out toward the last remnant of warmth.

Thomas knew he could tiptoe past and climb the stairs, but that would only put off the inevitable. Better to get it over with now while he felt awful. At least life couldn't get much worse than it already was. So he banged a pan on the stove top, banged it again until his father stirred. He came awake slowly, with much lip smacking and scratching beneath his britches. With luck he'd caught something down there that would fester and itch even worse.

"Tom." His eyes were slits. "Is there ale in the pantry?"

"I'll look." Though he knew there was. He poured some into a flagon and brought it through. His father drained half in one swallow, then looked once more at Thomas, noticing for the first time his state.

"You're wet," he said. Looked again. "And your face is purple in places." He nodded. "You did good last night. Took your beating like a man." A grin. "Did some damage of your own, too. They'll think twice before coming at you a second time." John Berrington sat straighter. "Maybe you're not so much the scholar I feared you were."

"I've lost the note, Pa," Thomas said.

"Note? What note?"

"Arthur Wodall's note of promise. Sixty shillings for the sheep. I've lost it. Or had it stolen. It's gone, anyway." Thomas spoke fast, the words spilling from him, trying to get them out before the inevitable. Which came almost immediately.

John Berrington rose, his stupor forgotten. "What do you mean, lost it?"

"The boys pushed me in the river, Pa, and the note got wet. I made a copy, but that's gone too now."

"Sixty shillings! You've cost me sixty shillings, you snivelling cur." His father loosened his leather belt, drawing it through his closed fists. "Come here, you little turd."

Thomas stepped back at the same time his mother emerged from the foot of the stairs.

"What's going on here? John, why have you your belt out?"

"This little shit has lost my note of promise."

"He showed it to me, but he said he had a plan."

"I did, Ma, but the copy's gone as well."

"You made a copy?" John Berrington had only now heard what Thomas said. "You made a copy of the note? You know that's against the law, don't you?"

"I didn't know what else to do, Pa."

John Berrington's eyes narrowed. "Can you make another?"

"I don't know. I remember the words, I think, but whether Brother Bernard will help again…"

"You went to the Priory for help? I always thought you were stupid, Tom, but that beats anything you've done before. Monks are men of God, lad, they don't hold with forgery."

"Brother Bernard's different. He's seen the world."

"I've still a mind to take the skin off your backside," said John Berrington, and his wife moved to place herself between the pair. As she did so, two more figures appeared at the foot of the stairs. Thomas's two-year-old sister Angnes in the arms of John Berrington the younger, who leaned against the door jamb to enjoy the entertainment.

"Lay a finger on me," Thomas said, "and I'll not even try to forge another note." He stared at his father. "Sixty shillings, Pa. Think on that."

John Berrington's face grew even redder than usual and he took a step forward, not a man to be told what he could or couldn't do, particularly not by his son. He stopped when his wife placed a hand against his chest.

"Look at him, John, he's black and blue already. And he means what he says."

"So do I. Fuck the sixty shillings, I won't allow any son of mine to talk to me that way." John Berrington pushed his wife aside and advanced on Thomas, who backed away at the look in his father's eyes. He'd taken a good beating the night before, been knocked senseless, but he saw murder in the man's eyes.

Thomas turned and ran.

He made it as far as the front door, swung it open and ran out into the arms of Hugh Gifforde. Thomas pushed away, stepping back into the kitchen.

"He's took his punishment already, Hugh, we all saw it. There's no need for anything more. Not unless you want to fight me as well." But Thomas saw his father look in puzzlement at the small group gathered on the stoop. Arthur Wodall stood there as well, together with Brother Bernard, all their faces grim. This had nothing to do with the beating evident on Thomas's face.

"Tom needs to come with us," said Hugh Gifforde.

"Why? I already said he took his beating, and that's an end of it. You have a problem with that, you better take it up with me, not him." The threat to one of his family had switched John Berrington's anger to a new target.

"This is nothing to do with what happened in the square," said Hugh Gifforde. "Not directly, in any case." He stepped aside, glancing back at Brother Bernard, who came forward.

"Take your shirt off, Tom," he said.

"Why?" Thomas didn't like the look in Brother Bernard's eyes. They showed none of the warmth he was used to.

"Do as I say instead of questioning me."

Thomas glanced around; his was father stone-faced, his mother pale. His brother John was smiling, bouncing Angnes on his arm, she with a thumb in her mouth. Thomas pulled his shirt over his head, revealing the marks on his body, more purple showing than white.

"Hold your hands out," said Brother Bernard, and Thomas obliged. The monk took them, leaning close to examine the knuckles. He looked up at Hugh Gifforde and nodded.

"Thomas Berrington," said Hugh Gifforde, moving forward again, "you stand accused of the murder of Raulf Wodall. You are to come with me now to the Priory, where you will be questioned and locked up until such time as you come to trial."

CHAPTER SIX

There were arguments, of course. John Berrington was full
of protective bluster as he stood on protocol. He pointed
out he was Sheriff of the area and as such it was his responsibility to decide on the guilt or not of an accused man. But
he knew he had a weak argument and soon backed down.
Once they reached the town, Prior Robert Goldston
pointed out that he, as the representative of God in
Lemster, was the ultimate judge. None of which affected
Thomas, who knew nothing of the arguments. He had been
taken to a monk's cell and the door locked.

The cell was small, with a horsehair mattress laid on a
narrow bedframe. There was no chair or table. A high
window, too narrow to squeeze through, was set in one
wall. It offered a view, when Thomas stood on the end of
the bed on tiptoe, of the water meadow, the Lugge, and
beyond to Eaton Hill where his family would be gathered in
the manor house. He wondered if his father believed him
innocent or had protected him out of habit. Was he even
now plotting some means of disavowing his son? Thomas
knew he was in trouble. He wished he knew how much, and

who his accuser was. He had witnessed hangings and knew it wasn't a pleasant way to die.

Thomas lay on the hard bed and closed his eyes. His head ached from the blow it had taken, but he was tired enough that sleep came, a refuge from the thoughts that threatened to engulf him.

When he woke, a splash of sun was in his eyes and his clothes had dried. He sat up, rubbing his palms across his face, wincing each time he encountered a cut or bruise. He needed to piss, but there was nowhere in the cell. He hammered on the door, shouted. Nothing.

He stood on the bed and peered through the window. He heard the sound of voices raised in prayer. It must be noon, which told Thomas he had slept a full five hours.

He dropped back onto the bed, pulled his knees to his chest and waited. He tried to think of something other than the pressure on his bladder. Eventually the chanting stopped. Soon after, footsteps passed the door and Thomas rose and hammered again.

A voice came, muffled through the dense wood, "What do you want?"

"I have to piss," Thomas shouted.

"Hold it. I'll fetch Brother Bernard."

Thomas called out again, but whoever was on the other side had gone. He sat again to wait, not sure if he could. Long, lazy minutes passed before he heard a key in the lock. The door opened and the tall figure of Brother Bernard entered.

"I hear you need to piss," he said. He untied the rope that cinched his robe at the waist and Thomas frowned. "Stand up, boy."

Boy now, was it? Thomas supposed an accusation of murder could do that. He stood.

Brother Bernard took Thomas's arms and held them out, his wrists gripped in a strong hand. The brother looped the rope around Thomas's wrists and tied a complex knot, then tugged at it to satisfy himself it wouldn't come loose. He looped the other end through his fist.

"Come on, then." He turned and Thomas trotted fast to keep up. Brother Bernard led him outside and along the side of the building where the monks slept. The smell alerted Thomas where they were going.

"I can piss outside," he said, but Brother Bernard dragged him into the fetid interior of the communal privy. One brother sat at the far end, his robe pulled up around his waist. He nodded affably to the pair of them.

"You might want to shit as well," said Brother Bernard. "I don't want you shouting the place down again in an hour." He nodded at holes cut in a length of oak that ran above the cesspit. "Do your business and let's get out of here."

Thomas squatted, but he only needed to piss, the sound loud in the confines of the privy. When he was done, Brother Bernard dragged him away, moving slower now.

"You can't believe I did this, can you?" Thomas said.

"It's not up to me to decide. The Prior is with Hugh Gifforde and your father now. A message has been sent to Hereford, but the matter will no doubt be decided here."

"I didn't kill anyone."

Brother Bernard slowed, stopped. He turned to face Thomas. The length of rope hung slack in his hand. Thomas glanced at it, thinking if he jerked hard enough it might come loose, and if he ran Brother Bernard wouldn't be able to catch him. But he waited to hear what the man had to say, curious. His father had always told him he was too curious, that it was bad for a boy to be so. Maybe he was right.

Instead of speaking, Brother Bernard shook his head and

tugged on the rope, turned in a different direction and dragged Thomas after him. He headed for the small infirmary, which as well as the library was his domain. Thomas had heard his tales of southern Spain and the wonderful knowledge the surgeons there possessed; knowledge far in advance of anything in England. Thomas hadn't believed him. He was like his father in that, at least. England was the centre of the world.

Brother Bernard pulled out another key, inserted it in the door and turned. Two locked doors in a single day. Thomas had never seen such in the Priory before.

Another tug and he was inside, and there was Raulf Wodall lying naked on a slab, his body paler than it had any right to be.

"See what you've done?" said Brother Bernard. He tugged at the rope so the knot bit into Thomas's wrists, drawing him closer. "See this? This is where a knife entered him. And here, and here, and here. This blow killed him, but the others would have done so given time."

"Where was he found?" Thomas wasn't afraid of the body, nor upset at the presence of death or sight of the wounds. "Was it a big knife?"

"Big enough to kill him. And he was found at the foot of Cursneh Hill."

"That's well over a mile west of town," Thomas said. "What was Raulf doing all the way out there? He lives not so far from me."

"That's what the Prior might want to ask you. What you were doing out there as well. If he wants to talk to you at all."

"I didn't do this."

"Do you deny you fought him yesterday? That you threw him in the Lugge?"

"No."

"Do you deny you were attacked last night in the town square and Raulf Wodall was one of the attackers?"

"It was the Giffordes did this to me." Thomas pointed at his face. "And I was attacked again while I walked home, near the place we had that first fight. Attacked and meant to drown. So maybe whoever hit me is the same person who killed Raulf."

"Except you weren't stabbed. Even if I was to believe someone attacked you. And why the same person? Raulf at Cursneh Hill, you on your way to Eaton. That's a distance nearer two miles than one. Who would travel such a distance to attack two boys?"

"Why ask me? I didn't see who it was, but this lump on the back of my head is proof enough."

Brother Bernard shook his head. "Everyone saw you in the square. Half the town saw what the Giffordes did to you. That lump on your skull could be from that fight, or maybe the fight on the oak bridge."

Thomas stared at Raulf's body. He was sorry to see him dead, even though he had never particularly liked him. He supposed his chances with Susan Wodall would be spoiled now. She would want nothing to do with him if she believed he had killed her brother. Not unless he could prove his innocence. Better still if he could prove the guilt of whoever carried out the attack on her brother.

"Symon Dawbney had a knife," Thomas said.

"Every boy has a knife. Even you, I expect." Thomas could almost feel the weight of Brother Bernard's gaze as it crawled across him. "Take your shirt off, Thomas."

He took a step back. "Why? I already did that once."

Brother Bernard reached out fast and slapped Thomas about the ear. "Don't ask why, just do as I say."

Thomas shook his head. Brother Bernard pulled at the cord, drawing him closer, and even though Thomas fought, the monk was too strong. He had been a soldier not so long ago and had lost none of his strength. When he was within reach, Brother Bernard grasped Thomas's shirt and pulled until it ripped.

"Now your breeches."

"What?"

"God's teeth, Thomas, how can a boy as clever as you be so stupid? Do you want me to slap you again?"

"I don't want you to do anything to me." He glanced at Raulf. Had Brother Bernard killed him? Was he about to kill Thomas as well to hide his secret? He pulled away, but Brother Bernard failed to give an inch.

"Do you want me to tear those off you as well?"

Thomas shook his head, knowing he was trapped. He stopped pulling and came a little closer. He untied his breeches and let them drop. He stood there, naked. Brother Bernard's eyes took him in from head to toe. He twirled a finger and Thomas turned around.

"You can put them back on now."

Thomas frowned. "What was that for?"

"They gave you a good beating, didn't they?"

"Not as good as they wanted." Thomas picked up his breeches and pulled them up, tied the cord at his waist. His shirt would hang open from the tear, but he pulled it on as well as he could. "I could do with a bit of rope to tie this up with," he said.

Brother Bernard smiled. "I expect you could."

Thomas glanced at Raulf again. It was difficult not to, him just lying there all pale, his chest punctured with wounds.

"Do you truly think I killed him?"

It was Brother Bernard's turn to look. He sighed. "It's not up to me whether you did or not. And God sees all. If they hang you, He will ensure if you are innocent, you will be given swift admittance to heaven."

"I'd rather stay down here if it's all the same to God." Thomas ducked as Brother Bernard's hand flicked out. He was fast enough this time, or the man was no longer trying.

"Let us suppose for a moment," said Brother Bernard, "that you did not kill Raulf." He stared hard at Thomas. "Have you any idea who might have?"

"How long have you got?"

"Was he not popular?"

Thomas shook his head.

"But he was a lad. Lads aren't meant to be likeable. But they're not hated either, in general. They are simply there is all, until they're old enough to cause more serious trouble, and then it's marriage, the army or the church for most."

"Which is it for me, Bernard?"

Another flick of the wrist, but he was barely trying now. "You, I suspect, are destined for none of those. If, that is, you are not destined for the rope. At the moment that looks the most likely."

"Am I likeable?" Thomas asked. It wasn't something he'd ever given much thought to, expect when it came to Susan Wodall, and that was spoiled now. He gave another glance toward her brother, but he was still as pale, still as dead as the last time he looked. "When will he be buried?"

"Tomorrow morning. His family have a plot next to the house so he'll be laid there. The Prior says he'll go out and say the prayers. And yes, you're likeable enough, though quite why I can't say. You're not like the other boys, are you?" Brother Bernard looked around. He found a chair and pulled it across, offered it to Thomas, then took another for himself. So they were staying a while, it seemed.

"Am I not? Pa hits me often enough, so I thought I was just like everyone else."

"I suspect your father's not exactly sure what to do with you."

"Then it's lucky I have a brother. He's just like Pa. Pa doesn't hit John, not anymore."

"I hear John Talbot is calling his squires together. He wants an army for France. There are rumours of pestilence in some towns so I suspect he's holding back to see if it spreads. Like as not your brother John will go with your father across the sea to fight. You'll be the man of the house then. It will make a proper man of you, no doubt."

"If I don't swing first."

"Aye, there is that." Brother Bernard glanced at Raulf. "I want you to do something for me."

"What?" Thomas was suspicious again. Bernard had always been proper with him, but he'd heard tales from other boys his age that not all the monks were as correct.

"I want you to take a look at Raulf. A good look. Get close and tell me what you see."

"Why?"

"Let's just say I'm curious."

Thomas shook his head at the notion, but he stood and walked as far as the rope tied to his wrist allowed. He stopped and looked down at it. Brother Bernard let loose his hold and Thomas continued to the wooden bench. He looked at the boy who had never been his friend. He tried to think if any of the boys in town were his friends, but came up short.

"Look at him," Brother Bernard urged, still sitting. Thomas knew he could run now if he wanted. He was

47

closer to the door, and he had a suspicion Brother Bernard wouldn't try too hard to stop him. The idea was tempting. Instead, he leaned over and got close to the body of Raulf Wodall.

"Can I touch him?"

Brother Bernard nodded.

Raulf's flesh was cold and waxy. When Thomas tried to move the hand to examine the palm, he found it stiff, difficult to turn.

"It's rigor," said Brother Bernard. "If it has reached his hands it means he's been dead ten hours, near as like."

"Which would make it some time after midnight, but before dawn," Thomas said, and Brother Bernard nodded. "I was out cold in the Lugge then."

"So you say."

"Everyone saw my clothes were all wet."

A smile. "Well that proves it, then, doesn't it?"

"He's got a cut right through his palm," Thomas said, laying the hand flat and pointing.

"I saw it."

Thomas held his own hands up, as if protecting himself from a blow or a knife, and Brother Bernard nodded. "Good. Now look harder."

Thomas did, but the mark was still a cut and told him nothing more. He started to examine the arms and found more marks. He came to the chest. Five puncture wounds. One on the right side that was shallow but long. Two to the belly. Thomas drew the edges apart, fascinated when he glimpsed coils of intestine within.

"You're not squeamish, are you?" said Brother Bernard.

"I've helped slaughter pigs, sheep and cattle. I know what's inside a body. Us and the animals are all the same under the skin."

"Except in here." Brother Bernard tapped his skull. "We have minds, all the better to appreciate God's glory." He tapped his chest. "And we have souls, all the better to worship Him."

"Is that where the soul lies?" Thomas said.

"I don't know. Some scholars say it does, other claim it isn't a thing but more a state of mind. I'm still waiting. Which blow killed him?"

"Either of those to the belly would," Thomas said, straightening. "But they'd take time." He placed his fingers over an incision slightly left of centre on the chest. "I reckon this is what did for him."

Brother Bernard offered a soft nod. "Very good. Why?"

"His heart, of course."

"And the other blows? Were they before or after the one that killed him?"

"I can't tell."

"Why not?"

"Can you?"

"I want to hear your opinion. It is not me who is accused of murder, remember."

"He wasn't found this way, was he?" Thomas said. "Somebody's washed him, cleaned away the blood. If it had been left, I might be able to tell which of the wounds bled the most."

Another nod. "Good. Yes, good. It was me who cleaned him. His parents wanted to see him and I couldn't let them with him in the state he was found."

"Who was it found him? And which were the first blows?"

"The strike to his belly was the first, then his hand when he raised it to protect himself. The heart was, I believe, the final blow."

"You could tell all of that?"

"There was a lot of blood when I was taken to him. Blood can tell you a great deal if you know what you're looking for. And it was Joan Brickenden found him on her way home from The Star. It fair gave her a fright, and Joan's seen some sights in her time." Brother Bernard turned at a knock against the side of the door. One of the younger monks stood there, a look of uncertainty about him.

"What is it, Brother Mark?"

"They're ready for him now, sir."

"What have I told you? Don't call me sir. We are all brothers here, equal under God."

"Yes, sir. But they still want him."

Brother Bernard nodded. "Then go tell them we are coming."

CHAPTER SEVEN

Three men sat behind a long table that looked as if it had been brought in from the refectory, Prior Robert Goldston at their centre. On his left was Hugh Gifforde. To his right sat the Earl of Shrewsbury's man, Peter Markel. It was not his place to offer judgement in Lemster, but he was a man of substance, and with Thomas's father forfeiting his place, it had fallen to the most senior figure available. Peter Markel must have extended his stay especially. Two other men stood to one side: John Berrington and Arthur Wodall, a good distance between them. Thomas could see his father's impatience in the way he shifted from foot to foot, and how his eyes flickered between those seated at the table.

Thomas stood near the back of the room, Brother Bernard beside him, the length of cord still laid across his hand. It was not gripped, but Thomas knew there was no escaping it.

"Who speaks for the boy?" asked Prior Robert Goldston.

Thomas glanced at his father, but it seemed he would not. Instead, Brother Bernard said, "I speak for Thomas Berrington."

Prior Goldston looked toward John Berrington, returned his gaze to Thomas, and then Brother Bernard. "Are you sure? Is such allowed?"

Thomas would have expected the Prior, as arbiter of justice in the town, to know such things, though his judgement was not often called on. Thomas barely remembered the last time a murder had been committed in Lemster.

"I believe it is, Your Grace," said Brother Bernard.

"He is right," said Peter Markel. If anyone in the room knew the rules of judgement, it would be him.

"Are you sure?" Prior Goldston remained uncertain.

"I believe the accused can ask any man to represent him. I recall no mention of their profession or calling, so long as they are men of substance and experience. And I believe Brother Bernard has a great deal of experience. As much as any man in this room."

Thomas caught a look pass between the two. He knew Brother Bernard had fought in Spain—had Peter Markel done so too? Or in some other campaign?

Peter Markel's word appeared to be enough. The Prior cleared his throat. "How plead you, Thomas Berrington? Guilty or no?"

"Not guilty," Thomas said, making an effort to still the tremor in his voice as he replied.

"And who accuses him?"

"I do." Arthur Wodall took a step away from his position at the wall, firming his shoulders. His face was grey, lined by grief. He refused to look at Thomas.

"On what proof?" asked Prior Goldston.

"Proof? I need no proof. Everyone knows he tossed my son in the Lugge. Walter Gifforde and Symon Dawbney were there, they saw him do it."

"And where are these boys now? Why are they not here to confirm the accusations?"

"They have been sent for," said Arthur Wodall. "But everyone knows it was Tom Berrington killed my boy. Words are cheap, it's actions that count. And I demand action. This…" he raised a hand, even then refusing to look toward Thomas, "…creature must account for his actions. I demand it. The whole of the town demands it."

"Does it?" said Prior Goldston. He looked to Brother Bernard. "Have you heard word of such demands, brother?"

A shake of the head.

"Why are the boys who make this accusation not here?"

"They ought to be outside by now, Your Grace."

"Then bring them in. I want to see their faces when they tell me what they witnessed."

Arthur Wodall went to the door and passed through.

"If I know boys," said Peter Markel, "they'll have disappeared in search of mischief."

But they had not. Whether due to fear of the Prior or fear of what others might think of their accusations, they had been waiting outside and were now ushered in. Symon Dawbney's gaze remained on the ground beneath his feet, but Walter Gifforde's took in the seated men, those standing against the wall, and came to rest on Thomas. A sly smile crossed his face, but he suppressed it before anyone else saw it. Thomas returned a stare filled with malevolence, pleased to see Walter's gaze falter.

Prior Goldston beckoned the pair to come stand in front of the table. Walter went willingly enough, Symon shuffling along until he stopped a foot further back.

"You know that what you say here is said in front of God Almighty, do you not?" said the Prior.

Walter nodded, and after a moment, Symon followed suit.

"Good. So tell me what you saw that would indicate Thomas Berrington is guilty of the murder of Raulf Wodall."

It was the first time Thomas had heard the words spoken in such a way and a chill ran through him. *Guilty of murder!* That was the accusation made, that he had deliberately killed another boy. He examined the faces of the men behind the table and saw no mercy there. When he glanced in the direction of his father, he saw even less.

"He picked the fight," said Walter Gifforde. "We were doing nothing and he came right onto the tree and punched poor Raulf and knocked him straight into the Lugge. Thomas knows Raulf don't swim. Wanted to kill him, he did. Got to him after, must have." The words came out in a rush, as if Walter could only hold them straight in his head so long and wanted rid of them.

"Why would Thomas want to kill Raulf?" asked Prior Goldston. "Was there bad blood between them?"

"Bad blood between him and everyone." Walter pointed at Thomas. His finger shook, and after a moment he lowered it and held it inside his other hand.

Prior Goldston turned his attention to Symon Dawbney. He motioned him forward, and after a long moment, Symon took a single step before coming to a halt.

"Did you see the same thing?" asked Prior Goldston, his voice soft.

Symon nodded, and kept on nodding.

"You will need to tell us what you saw."

"Thomas hit him. Hit Raulf. Right on the nose."

"Why would he do that?" It wasn't the Prior who asked the question, but Peter Markel. "Why would Thomas Berrington attack Raulf without provocation?"

54

"It's what he does," said Walter, which set Symon to nodding once more. "Bad to the bone, Tom is."

"Did either of you, or anyone else, see Thomas with Raulf on the night he died?"

"Was dark," said Walter. "He could've been anywhere."

"But he was..." Peter Markel consulted a note written in front of him, "in the market square at a little after nine, where he got into a fight with the Giffordes. Is that not so?"

"Like I said, Tom's always fighting."

Peter Markel looked toward Thomas. "Is this true, Thomas? Are you always fighting?"

Thomas shook his head. "To look at me now, you wouldn't know it, but I don't fight 'less I have to."

Prior Goldston sat back and folded his arms across his ample belly, glad for someone else to be taking control.

Peter Markel looked between Walter and Symon, judging them.

He turned his gaze on Thomas as he pointed to Symon. "Surely you cannot beat him in a fair fight, can you?" It must have been obvious to him Walter would have offered even less of a threat.

"He's big, but he's slow," said Thomas.

"So you have fought him?"

"When I had to. Nobody expects me to stand around and let him hit me, do they?"

"How often?" asked Peter Markel.

"Not often. A few more times of late, but only because they are always together. I think they put each other up to it."

"The three of them?" asked Peter Markel, and Thomas nodded. "Why would they do that? Why would they direct their attentions at you and not someone else?"

"Oh, they do," Thomas said. "But I'm..." He hesitated.

Glanced at his father, who was staring at Peter Markel with a frown, perhaps unable to fathom why he was listening to what his son had to say. His son the murderer.

"What are you?"

"I'm Thomas Berrington," Thomas said, as though it was obvious, but he saw he needed to add more. Not for Peter Markel perhaps, but for the others who wouldn't see it. "I am my father's son. John Berrington's son, who serves your master. He has a position in this town, and that makes his sons targets. We are fair game. My brother had the same trouble I do, but he's too big now. Nobody picks on John anymore."

"But they pick on you?"

Thomas lifted a shoulder. "Sometimes."

"And Raulf picked on you? Is that what you're saying? Raulf picked on you, so you killed him?"

"I didn't kill anybody!"

"Except a boy is dead and his friends say there was bad blood between the two of you."

"That's a lie!" Thomas felt anger surge through him and tried to damp it down, knowing it would do him no good. He failed, and having failed gave full rein to it. "If anyone killed him it was Symon there. They were always falling out."

"We was not!" said Symon.

"It was Tom," said Walter. "Raulf's sister says she saw him following Raulf along Green Lane."

Peter Markel turned his head. His eyes were sharp flints in their sockets, grey and cold and questioning. "Raulf's sister? That would be…" Once more he referred to his notes, "Susan?"

Walter nodded. "She said she saw Raulf talking with Bel

Brickenden on Green Lane, and everyone knows Tom holds a flame for Bel."

Peter Markel smiled. "Like more than half the men in Lemster, I hear. Is this true, Tom?"

A shake of the head. "I like her well enough, but not that way, sir." He thought it worth throwing in a sir here and there.

Peter Markel looked Thomas up and down, his gaze slow. "Have you been with a girl, Tom?"

The question made Thomas frown. It was irrelevant to the accusation against him, but he answered anyway. "No." He laid a hand over his heart. "I swear to God I been with no girl never."

"What age are you?"

"I have thirteen years, sir."

"And you've not been with a girl yet?" Peter Markel glanced toward John Berrington. "Are you saving the boy for someone special, John?"

"I offered," said John Berrington. "I offered last night. Told him he should go upstairs with Jilly, but he turned me down."

"Is this true, Tom?"

A nod. "It is, sir."

"And you didn't go?"

"I hadn't the penny, sir."

Peter Markel started to laugh. Even Prior Goldston's lips showed a curl.

"Is that what she charges, a penny? Well damn me, if I'd known that I'd have tumbled her myself. She's a sweet little thing."

Thomas was aware events were slipping into areas that had nothing to do with his guilt or innocence.

Peter Markel, perhaps appreciating the same, pulled himself together and made an effort to restore his stern expression. "Has anyone thought to bring this Bel Brickenden here? The body of Raulf Wodall was found on Cursneh Hill, was it not? That is on the roadway toward her house, I believe. She might be a witness, and she's not been called?"

"The family sleeps late, I am told," said Hugh Gifforde, his first contribution to the interrogation; such as it was.

Peter Markel glanced toward the windows, clear glass set high in the walls. "It is near to noon. Send for the girl and we will take some food." He looked toward Prior Goldston. "If that is acceptable, Your Grace?"

The other boys fled like the devil was on their heels. Within moments, Thomas found himself between two men: Brother Bernard, who had taken the end of the rope which he remained tied to, and his father, who slapped him hard around the back of the head.

"What were you thinking of, Tom, killing that boy?"

"Now, John, we're still looking at the proof of that," said Brother Bernard.

Thomas rubbed his scalp.

"I didn't kill anyone. And you should believe me, Father, not go listening to rumour."

All the protest did was bring a second slap, harder than the first.

"I'd let them hang you now if it wouldn't show me in a bad light."

"Thomas claims he is innocent," said Brother Bernard, but John Berrington ignored him.

"Why did you do it? If you wanted to kill someone, you could have picked a better target, somebody more worthy. A girl could have killed Raulf Wodall."

"I didn't kill him." Thomas stepped back as his father

raised his hand again, but no slap came and he was brought up short by the rope.

John Berrington shook his head. "I'm going to eat with the others, see if I can come to some kind of arrangement." He shook his head again and left the room.

Brother Bernard tugged at the rope and Thomas tugged back.

"Do you doubt me too?"

"I have no opinion on the matter, but I need to put you back in your cell."

"I want to see Raulf again," Thomas said.

"Why?" Brother Bernard stared at Thomas, his expression showing nothing of his thoughts.

"Just want to, is all."

"Not good enough. Give me a reason and I might allow it."

"I don't know a reason other than I want to see him, to look close again to see if there's something I missed."

Brother Bernard smiled. "Something I missed, do you mean?"

"How close did you look?" Thomas said.

"Close enough." Brother Bernard shook his head, sighed. "But if that's what you want, I can't see the harm in it. The others will be an hour at least, more like two." He tugged at the rope and led Thomas out into the May sunshine, tart with the scent of lavender from the Priory gardens.

* * *

"So, did you learn anything you didn't know before?" Brother Bernard had sat the whole time on a chair, watching as Thomas leaned close to examine Raulf Wodall's corpse.

Thomas held up Raulf's right hand. "He's got skin under his nails, and one's been snapped off completely."

"He's a boy," said Brother Bernard. "Boy's break nails all the time. Even you, I expect. What does it tell you?"

"That he fought. That he might have scratched whoever killed him."

"He fought you not four hours before he was killed. Like as not it's your skin under his nails, though how anyone could prove it is beyond knowing."

Thomas opened the loose flaps of his own shirt. "So where are the scratches, Bernard?"

There was no correction of the informality. "Under those bruises maybe, who can tell?"

"You can, I know you can. You made me strip and you looked me all over and you would have seen any scratches. You saw his nails before I did and that's why you wanted me naked, wasn't it?"

Brother Bernard gave no indication one way or the other.

"We're looking for someone with scratches," Thomas said. He had seen all he could of Raulf's wounds, extracted all the information he was capable of taking from the body.

Brother Bernard laughed and motioned Thomas closer. He held out his hand. Thomas lifted the rope and handed the end to him.

"When was the last time you pushed through a hedge, Thomas? Everyone's got a scratch or two on them, even me." He lifted the sleeve of his robe to show a red weal along his forearm. "I got this working in the garden only yesterday. Half the monks have similar marks on them."

"I haven't."

"Is that meant to prove your innocence?"

"No. The fact I didn't kill Raulf proves my innocence."

"That is not for me to decide."

Thomas made a dismissive sound. "What—do you

honestly believe the men in that room can decide fairly? They couldn't find their arses 'less they sat on their own hands."

Thomas didn't see Brother Bernard move, only felt a slap against his face that brought tears to his eyes. When he blinked them away, Brother Bernard appeared unchanged, his soft brown eyes staring into Thomas's.

"You are talking of my Prior, the Earl of Shrewsbury's trusted agent, and Hugh Gifforde, who is respected in this town. You are talking of the men who will decide your fate. Take care what you say, and who you say it to."

Thomas shook his head, refusing to apologise. He had meant what he said about the men. Except for Peter Markel, who wasn't stupid. But would that be enough? He was the Earl's man. All he cared for was how the accusation might reflect on, disadvantage, or advantage his master. The fact that Thomas's father John Berrington was the Earl's squire didn't help.

"Are you a virgin, Thomas?" asked Brother Bernard.

Thomas was confused. "What kind of question is that? I could as well ask the same for you."

"Except I am a full-grown man who has travelled the world, while you are just coming into your manhood. And the question has relevance. Humour me, Thomas. Are you a virgin?"

"What if I am? It's not another crime, is it?"

"Indeed it is not, otherwise many of us would be for the gallows, even men of God such as most of the brothers."

"Except you said you had a life before coming here."

A smile. "Indeed I did. A rich, exciting and often dangerous life. Which is one of the reasons I came here. Lemster Priory suits a man who might have seen more of the world than is good for him. Bear that in mind when you are full grown. All men have choices if they can only see them. Try to make the right choices."

Thomas shook his head. "Does it matter? That I'm a virgin?"

"Two reasons I asked." Brother Bernard held up his left hand, the fist closed until he released his index finger. "If you are not a virgin then you might know a little about women. And women are often the cause of a falling out between men. Or violence. Bel Brickenden is a girl of rare beauty, is she not? Some would want to clasp her to their breast and keep her to themself."

"I never went with her!" Thomas said. "She doesn't even look at me."

"But you are tempted, aren't you? And even if she doesn't look at you, that doesn't stop you looking at her, does it? Did you kill Raulf because you saw him talking to her on Green Lane? Or were they doing more than talking?"

Thomas looked at Brother Bernard's hand. "I don't suppose there's much point in me telling you I wasn't talking to Bel, is there? What's the other reason?"

A second finger joined the first. "Some men who have not enjoyed the pleasure of a woman still lust after it mightily. That lust can twist their mind until it turns to thoughts of violence instead of love."

"But it wasn't Bel who was attacked."

"No, indeed. But what if it was Raulf offering her protection? Why else was he so far out from town?" Brother Bernard stood and walked to the door. When the rope tied at his wrist drew taut, Thomas followed.

CHAPTER EIGHT

Thomas watched the shadows creep across the cell wall, trying to judge the passage of time. At one point he heard raised voices, the kind of raised voices that hinted at well-fed bellies and several flagons of mead and wine. He tried to consider whether it was to his advantage or not.

When Brother Bernard came for him, he was standing ready, his hands held out. The rope was noosed around his wrist and pulled tight.

Raulf and Symon seemed to have been dismissed, but Bel Brickenden stood in front of the long table. Everyone in the room knew the work Bel's mother did, and most expected Bel to follow in the same trade. It was unlikely any of those present judged her or her mother. It was well known that men married for status, money and convenience, but it was women like Joan Brickenden they came to when they had a need to spill their seed away from home. Whore, in Lemster at least, was a respected profession. Thomas was only sorry he hadn't had a penny the night before. Perhaps if he had, none of this would have happened, or at least he might not be about to hang a virgin.

"Do you know this boy?" asked Peter Markel, indicating Thomas with a nod of his head.

"'Course I know Tom." Bel smiled.

"Did you see him last night?"

Bel rolled her eyes. "Everyone saw him getting beat on by the Giffordes."

"After that?"

Bel smiled. "I went home after. Ma said she would be some time yet."

"What time did you walk home? Were you alone?"

"It was close to midnight. The Star was busy last night, what with both a market and the tinkers in town. And I was on my own, same as always. Everybody knows me and nobody gives me trouble. They wouldn't dare."

"Did you see Raulf Wodall on your way home?"

"I saw him earlier, of course I did, he was one of those beating on Tom, but I never saw him after that."

"So why did Susan Wodall say she saw you talking with her brother?"

"I don't know," said Bel, "only that I never did."

"Were you with your mother when she found Raulf's body?" asked Peter Markel, his eyes sharp on her.

A shake of the head. Bel's red-brown hair swayed, as did her budding breasts. Thomas's eyes tracked across her. Bel was dressed in a plain blouse with long sleeves, a skirt that reached half way between knee and ankle. When he looked closer, he saw scratches on her legs, as if she had forced her way through a bramble patch, or laid on one with some-body. Thomas glanced at Brother Bernard to see his eyes were also on Bel, but they might have been there for another reason altogether.

"I was asleep when Ma came home. Didn't even know it was her found poor Raulf until you said just now."

"Your mother didn't think to mention it to you? That seems strange, does it not?"

"To you, maybe, but Ma sleeps late. I was gone from the house before she was awake."

"And your father said nothing either?"

"Pa was working."

Peter Markel consulted the notes he had written.

"Did you see anyone else on your way home? Thomas Berrington, perhaps?"

"I already told you I never saw Tom. I wish I had, he might not be standing here if I did. The only person I saw was Lizzie Martin, crying fit to burst."

Peter Markel leaned forward. "Why was she crying?"

"Boys," Bel said, obviously reckoning no other explanation necessary, but Peter Markel had other ideas.

"What boys?"

"She wouldn't say."

"Did she say why they made her cry? And you did say boys, not boy, didn't you?"

"Boys is what Lizzie said. She told me what they done but swore me to keep it secret." Bel crossed her arms as if the matter was closed. It was true that Thomas liked Bel. She was sweet-natured and generous, and always had a kind word for him. He knew, for instance, that her father used to beat her but had stopped doing so a year ago. He knew Bel was thinking about following her mother into the same profession, but that her mother wanted better for her. Marriage to a man of status, perhaps.

"Thomas Berrington is accused of murder," Peter Markel said. "I think that important enough for you to tell us whatever secret it was Lizzie told you."

Bel glanced in Thomas's direction. Her eyes tracked him without judgement.

"Tom never killed no one," she said. "Tom would never kill anybody, he's not like that. Tom's got a head on him. He's clever as well as good-looking."

Bel thought him good-looking? That was news to Thomas.

"Then it's a pity you're not judging him," said Peter Markel. "What did Lizzie tell you? We are measuring a boy's life here, Bel. Secret or no, you must tell us whatever you know."

Bel's eyes studied the flagstones, her face grave.

"Promises are given to be kept, sir. And secrets are given to be kept, too."

Peter Markel washed a hand across his face and sighed. "You are close to getting yourself locked up as well. I offer you one last chance to tell us what happened to Lizzie."

Bel glanced at Thomas, then at his father and Arthur Wodall. They would not have been invited to eat with the others in case the matter at hand needed discussing. They would instead have walked into town to find a meal. Not together, though. Not after what Thomas was accused of.

Bel spoke, but her voice was too soft to carry.

"Speak up!" It was Prior Goldston. His face showed anger, but his eyes showed something else as they stared at Bel.

"She said three boys dragged her into some bushes alongside the Kenwater and tried to do things to her."

"Things?" Peter Markel had taken control again, which was a good thing, Thomas thought.

"Things she didn't want them to," said Bel.

"Can you describe these things?"

Bel raised her eyes, her spirit returning. "Do I need to, sir? Everyone knows what boys want to do with girls. That's what they wanted to do with Lizzie."

"Who were the boys?"

"She didn't say." Bel's eyes dropped again and she hunched her shoulders.

"You and this Lizzie are friends?"

"Some," said Bel. "I don't have many friends, not good friends, but we know each other."

"She would have told you who the boys were, I am sure."

"Didn't know, she said. It was too dark, and there were the brambles. They caught at my legs when I helped her out of them."

Peter Markel shook his head and glanced at Brother Bernard. "Send for this Lizzie Martin, have her brought here." When Brother Bernard had gone out to find someone to fetch the girl, Peter Markel turned back to Bel. "I think you know, girl. I think you know full well who attacked Lizzie Martin, and when I find out the truth there is going to be trouble for you."

Bel met his stare but said nothing. Thomas knew it was a false threat being made. Peter Markel knew full well any punishment attempted against the daughter of Joan Brickenden would bring down the ire of half of Lemster.

The questioning had reached a pause so Thomas was returned to his cell. Brother Bernard left the rope tied at his wrist, a sign they wouldn't be there long. Thomas expected the monk to leave, but instead he hitched up his robe and sat on a stool across from the narrow cot.

"What will they do?" Thomas asked. "Take me direct to be hung, or draw it out? I think if they're going to do it, I'd rather it be done quick."

"Who says you're going to hang?"

Thomas made a show of looking around the cell. "Do you see anyone else in here?"

"The girl might know something," said Brother Bernard.

"Arthur Wodall's looking to punish someone and he doesn't much care who it is."

"Have you considered he might want honest justice for the death of his son?"

Thomas didn't consider the comment warranted a reply. Instead he picked at the rope on his wrist. It was starting to chafe.

"Bel Brickenden knows more than she's saying," said Brother Bernard.

"Bel's Ma knows all the secrets in town and more besides. I expect she talks to Bel about some of them."

"So why doesn't she tell us what she knows?"

"She's loyal. Maybe when Lizzie gets here they'll get a chance to talk and Bel can persuade her."

"She likes you," Brother Bernard said.

"Lizzie does?"

Brother Bernard offered a smile. "Bel, idiot."

Thomas laughed. "I don't think so. Bel was being kind, that's all. She does that all the time."

"I think you may get to sleep in your own bed tonight, Tom."

"What makes you say that?"

"They are going around in circles. Until someone comes forward and says they saw you strike the blow, there is no proof and they know it. Your father is an important man, not just in this town but all through the Marches. And Peter Markel is the Earl's man, same as John Berrington. It wouldn't look good to let the town see you hang, even if you did kill Raulf." Brother Bernard gazed at the high window, the brightness catching in his pale eyes. "You didn't kill him, did you?"

"Do you need to ask?"

Brother Bernard shrugged as if he didn't care one way or

68

another. He reached out and flicked the knot at Thomas's wrist. As if by magic the rope fell loose. Thomas drew his hands free, rubbing at the red marks on his skin.

"I know you won't run," said Brother Bernard, rising to leave.

Thomas smiled. "You're too trusting."

But Brother Bernard was right. An hour passed before a young monk came to tell Thomas he was free to go. The court had broken for the day and Thomas was told his father was waiting for him in the Priory garden.

John Berrington stood outside talking with a tall man who had visited their house on several occasions. Thomas wondered what John Talbot, Earl of Shrewsbury, was doing in Lemster. Had he heard his agent Peter Markel was conducting a trial instead of performing whatever duty he had been sent here for? Thomas stood at a distance, unwilling to interrupt. John Talbot was a man of position, a man of power, and he barely acknowledged Thomas's existence. Which was both right and just. Thomas couldn't help him in any way, and for John Talbot there was no purpose to anyone who couldn't fight for him or enrich him in some way. Unless they were female and willing. Thomas suspected the willing part was sometimes optional.

Thomas looked around the quadrangle but saw no sign of Bel. He wanted to talk to her, but knew if he wandered off now, his father would notice and it would result in a beating. Instead he waited, fighting his own impatience, wondering how he could get Bel alone. He wondered if Brother Bernard spoke true and Bel did indeed like him. It was a strange thought that sparked a heat in his body that came more and more frequently these days. Thomas knew he was changing, starting to grow into a man, with all a man's weaknesses and all a man's responsibilities. His responsibilities he hoped he might grow to accept, and his weaknesses he could overcome.

The thought of weaknesses made him look toward his father. He stood with feet spread, fists at his waist as John Talbot spoke at him. John Berrington scowled, but Thomas knew there was nothing he could do but listen. He wondered if his father was being berated, and if so for what.

John Talbot grasped his father's arm before turning away. He crooked a finger for Peter Markel to follow. John Berrington turned to find his son staring at him and Thomas felt his own shoulders tense, knowing what was coming. His father came toward him, his face as dark as thunder clouds over the Welsh hills, and Thomas knew he couldn't run.

John Berrington reached out and slapped him hard across the side of the head.

"Ow! What was that for?"

"What do you think it was for?"

"I didn't kill him," Thomas said.

"So you say. Sometimes I think it would be better if you had. At least it would show you're a man like your brother."

"Who's John killed, then?" Thomas fell into step beside his father as they moved away from the Priory toward the Ludlow road and the bridge across the Lugge. The few townsfolk who saw them avoided eye contact.

Thomas got another slap around the head.

"You'll damage my brain," he said.

"Too late for that. When we get home you've got chores to do, and then you're to help your mother with Angnes, and then you can go to your room. Stay there until I call for you in the morning for more chores. I need to keep you busy."

"Don't they want me tomorrow?" Thomas asked.

"The Earl needs Peter Markel in Shrewsbury on some business, but you're not off the hook yet. He says he'll be back the day after tomorrow to finish your judgement. The Prior has put a call out for men to serve as a jury."

"Do they believe I'm guilty?" Thomas thought about hanging. Thought about being dead, like Raulf was dead. He wondered if Brother Bernard was right and heaven existed. And if it existed, would there be a place for him there?

"Guilty or not doesn't matter. You might have killed Raulf, but you're still my son, and nobody is going to hang any son of John Berrington."

"I didn't kill him!" Thomas ducked to avoid a third blow. He judged his father in a more reasonable mood when he didn't try for a fourth time.

Beyond the bridge, they turned south. On their right, the travellers' camp had been almost completely taken down, the field rutted by horses' hoofs and the wheels of carts. Only two tents remained. From one came the sound of a hacking cough and Thomas wondered who was sick.

CHAPTER NINE

Sunrise remained an hour away as Thomas rose from bed, dressed and eased open the small window of his room. He hesitated, listening. He could hear his father's snores. The entire house, perhaps the whole of Lemster, could hear John Berrington's snores. Which meant his mother was most likely awake too, but Thomas wasn't concerned whether she heard him or not. He eased one leg through the small window, then the rest of his body, twisting to allow himself passage. Beyond lay the tiled roof of a lean-to used to store wood, hay and the occasional sheep or pig awaiting slaughter. Thomas worked his way to the edge, then used a wooden upright to help him climb to the ground. Even in the dark it was easy. He had crept from his room this way a score of times before, but previously had always returned before the household was awake. Today he was sure he would not. Peter Markel was in Shrewsbury this day, but had promised to return on the morrow. Thomas had but this one day to discover who had killed Raulf.

The fields were damp with dew, and Thomas's legs

became soaked to the knee as he made his way toward town. Most windows remained dark and he saw only one other person, a drunken man weaving his way home. From the state of his clothes and hair, he looked like he must have slept most of his inebriation off in a doorway. A faint grey light began to form in the eastern sky as Thomas climbed the slope of Cursneh Hill—the final resting place of Raulf Wodall.

Thomas had no clear notion of why he wanted to see the spot Raulf had died, only that it was a need he couldn't ignore. Brother Bernard had allowed enough clues to emerge for Thomas to work out the place. What he didn't know was what had brought Raulf to this spot. A small copse of trees stood on the highest point, mostly birch but with a tall pine at the centre which stood above everything else. This was where Raulf had been killed. Thomas had been to this spot often enough before, but not on the night of the killing. From the top of the hill, low as it was, the town was clearly laid out. Each house and street was clearly marked out, as if drawn by a map-maker. Thomas turned his back on the town and examined the ground, but found nothing. There was disturbed ground everywhere. Raulf had died two days before and any spoor was now lost beneath the trampling of other feet, no doubt in recovery of his body.

Thomas turned and looked all around. The sky was lightening fast now, the short nights of late May giving only a few brief hours of total darkness. Already the town was clearer, and off to the west a curl of dark smoke rose into the sky from where Bel's father had lit fires beneath the kilns he would use to bake the hard red brick that had built half of Lemster's new houses and shops, and gave the man himself his name. Adam Brickenden was a man of few words, his lineage stretching back to a time when the local clay was first dug from the ground and fired in a kiln. His wife too carried her own family trade, one that her daughter Bel might or might not follow. In Lemster, whore wasn't a term of abuse. Joan Brickenden was well-respected, as her mother and aunt had been before her. She was not the only whore in town, but she was the prettiest, and it was rumoured the most skilled in pleasing a man. Bel had been passed down her mother's beauty, and thoughts of her made Thomas uneasy even as he began to descend the hill. He knew he should be returning home. It was still not too late to avoid a beating, but instead he was drawn to the west and the Brickenden house.

Thomas recalled Bel saying her mother slept late, but not this morning. She was hanging washing on a line in the garden, the first rays of the risen sun already making the wool and hemp cloth steam. She glanced up as Thomas approached and offered a wide smile.

"If you're looking for Bel, Tom, she's still abed."

Thomas felt his face flush bright red, knew Joan Brickenden had seen it as well when she suppressed a smile.

"They tell me you found Raulf's body," he said.

Joan Brickenden gave a nod, the humour draining from her face. "Aye, I did right enough. Fair gave me a shock I can tell you."

"What were you doing atop Cursneh Hill at midnight?" Thomas knew it was not his place to ask such questions, but he wasn't sure anyone else had and he wanted answers. If not answers, then at least some clarity.

"I thought I heard something. Somebody crying out, and I'm not one to ignore a cry for help."

"Did you hear that word? Help?"

Joan Brickenden shook her head, her hair swaying like Tom recalled Bel's swaying. Thick and dark and needing to be touched. "No, just someone crying out."

"You were brave to go up on your own. What if you were attacked, too?"

Joan Brickenden laughed. "Nobody would attack me. Besides, I can take care of myself."

"Was Raulf already dead when you found him?"

"He was. Lying there pale, with the moonlight on his face."

"Did you see anyone else?"

"Nobody."

"Heard anybody?"

"Only the wind in the trees. I knelt and checked Raulf, but it was clear he'd gone. Then I came back into town and left a message for the Prior. Couldn't think who else to tell. Your father perhaps, but the Priory was closer. Then I came home and went to bed." She stared at Thomas. "Do you believe me?"

Thomas nodded.

"Or do you think I had something to do with it?" Her face showed nothing.

"Of course not. Why would you?"

"Was it really Bel you came here to see, Tom, or did you come to question me?"

"Has anyone else been here asking?"

"Peter Markel did. He had the same questions you did, and I gave him the same answers."

"I did come here to see Bel, but I think I'd better leave now."

Joan Brickendedn smiled, like the sun emerging from

75

behind a dark cloud. "Don't go doing that, Tom. It's past time Bel was up. Go tell her the day's passing. Do you know where she sleeps?"

Thomas shook his head. How would be know such a thing, however much he might want to?

"She's got her own space above Adam's works. Go around the side and you'll see some steps."

Thomas started to turn away, a riot of emotions racing through him too fast for him to recognise any of them.

"Bel tells me they're accusing you of killing Raulf."

Thomas stopped, turning back slowly. He nodded.

"Don't they know you'd never do such a wicked thing? I know you, Tom. So does Bel." She offered a smile. "She likes you, do you know that? Talks about you a lot."

"She does?"

"Yes, she does. She told me you couldn't kill anyone."

"Depends, I expect, on who the someone was and whether they were trying to kill me, I suppose."

"Was Raulf trying to kill you?"

"No."

"There you go, then. Off you go to Bel. Tell her she's got chores waiting, but there's no rush if you want to talk a while." She offered Thomas some kind of meaningful look, but the meaning, if one had been intended, was entirely lost on Thomas.

Adam Brickenden offered an uninterested nod as Thomas crossed the open side of the works, turned and climbed a sturdy staircase set against the flank of the building. At the top, he rapped on a door and waited. No answer came and he was trying to decide whether to try again when he heard the sound of bare feet crossing the wooden floor, and then a lock being thrown. By the time he pushed it open

76

and entered the room, Bel was almost back in bed, her naked back displayed in a shaft of sunlight. Thomas stopped dead in his tracks. When Bel was fully covered, she gave a laugh.

"You can come closer, Tom, I don't bite. Not unless you want me to."

Thomas stared at her, his mouth half open.

"What, have you never seen a woman's bare backside before?"

"Only my sister's, and she only has two years. Yours was … different."

Bel gave another laugh. "Pleased to hear it, Tom. What are you here for if not to stare at me?" She patted the side of the bed, a solid structure with a well-filled mattress. Thomas wondered if she was already following in her mother's footsteps in this room. The idea didn't upset him. The opposite, in fact. Bel patted the bed again. "If you want to talk, you got to come and sit next to me, Tom. I promise to try and behave."

Thomas closed half the distance between them and stopped. Bel stared at him, waiting. For a moment, Thomas considered turning and fleeing as far and as fast as he could, but he had come here with questions and knew running was a coward's escape. Scared of Bel in this mood he might be, but he didn't want to be considered a coward. Men were judged by their actions, that he knew, so he closed the distance and sat on the edge of the bed. Bel's scent enveloped him and almost sent him back to his feet. It had another effect on him too, one he tried to hide by turning half away. This close to her, he could see the smooth texture of Bel's skin, the softness of her hair where it caught in a shaft of sunlight.

"So what do you want, Tom? To talk, or more?"

"Just talk. Is that all right, Bel?"

"I expect so. How long did Ma say you had?"

"She didn't. She told me it was past time you got up, though." Thomas held up a hand as Bel started to lower the blanket that covered her.

"She won't mind if I stay here a while, I expect." Bel slid further under the blanket and Thomas felt something relax inside himself, not sure he altogether wanted it to.

"I want to thank you for speaking up for me yesterday."

"You never killed Raulf, I know that."

"Not everyone thinks the same way." Thomas smiled. It felt strange to have a naked Bel Brickenden mere inches from him. "I don't suppose you know who did kill him, do you?"

Bel shook her head.

"I want to ask you about Lizzie."

"Here I am right in front of you and you want to talk about another girl? You've got a lot to learn about seduction, you know."

"I expect I do, and you know full well that's not what I meant."

Bel reached out and covered his hand with hers. "You're sweet, Tom, do you know that?"

"You might be the only one who thinks so. Did Lizzie really not tell you who the boys were who attacked her?"

"Of course she did. I expect I don't even need to tell you who they are, do I?" Bel hadn't removed her hand and now her fingers started to rub backward and forward across Thomas's wrist.

"It would help if you did, just so I'm sure."

"Why? It weren't them who killed poor Raulf, because he was with them."

78

"What about later? If they attacked Lizzie they might have attacked Raulf."

"Raulf didn't have what they wanted, not like Lizzie did. You tell me the names and I'll nod if you get them right."

"Symon Dawbney," Thomas said, and Bel offered a nod. She turned his hand over and twined her fingers through his. He could feel her pulling the hand toward her and resisted.

"Walter Gifforde. And Raulf too, you said? I didn't think about him being there, but it makes sense. So whoever attacked him, it must have been later."

"See, I said you knew who they were."

"I went up to Cursneh Hill before I came here, to look at where he was found. I can't think what took him up there to die."

"I don't suppose he went there to die, did he? I know why he went."

"You do?"

"I do."

"Are you going to tell me?"

"For a kiss I might."

"I don't have any money. Not a penny, not a ha'penny, not even a farthing."

"I'm not my ma, Tom. The kiss is free, because I like you. I like you a lot."

Thomas laughed. "You do know I'm near two years younger than you, don't you? It's going to be a while before I come into any money of my own. Never if my father has anything to do with it."

"You can come work for my pa. He says he needs help, and you're strong, I know you are."

"What about me? I might want to do more than make bricks."

"There's nothing wrong with bricks," said Bel. She continued to pull on his hand and Thomas knew what her intention was and continued to resist. Not enough to stop her altogether, but enough to slow the inevitable progress.

"I didn't say there was, but I know I want more. I like books and knowledge and other things. I need more than hard work all day long and sleep at night."

"What about the love of a good woman?"

Thomas made a show of looking around. "Wherever would I find one of those around here?"

Bel laughed and sat up so fast Thomas wasn't ready for what came next. She kissed his neck, then turned his face and kissed his mouth. Then she lay back and pulled the blanket up almost enough to cover herself. He wasn't sure whether he caught a glimpse of her charms or not.

"Oh, I could so love you, Thomas Berrington. But I wouldn't know what to do with a clever man. Well, I would, but I expect a clever man might want more than just that, wouldn't he?"

Thomas smiled. "You are more than enough for any man, Bel. Why did Raulf climb Cursneh Hill?"

"Because that's where he thought he might find Lizzie Martin again."

"Again?"

"He was sweet on her," said Bel.

"Was she sweet on him?"

"Like as not she was once, but not anymore. Not even before he got himself dead."

"Was that why Symon and Walter raped her?"

"Didn't get that far. I don't think they'd know how to, anyway. They was likely almost as scared as she was. They ran off when I shouted at them."

"You were brave," Thomas said. "They're both strong boys."

"I'm not afraid of anyone, not man nor boy. Men do what I say, not the other way around. Just like you kissed me because I wanted you to."

"I seem to recollect it was you kissed me," Thomas said.

"Riled me up, you did." Bel sighed. "It's been a long time since anyone managed to do that. You'd be a catch for a girl like me, Tom, but I know you're meant for greater things. You'll be someone important one day, you see if you're not, and when you are remember who told you that." She smiled. "Remember the girl who taught you how to pleasure a woman."

"I told you, Bel, I don't have any coin, not a one."

"And I already told you I need no coin." She drew the blanket down on one side to reveal the smooth, pale skin of her shoulder. "You can lie with me now if you want. I know you want to. I want it too. More than I've wanted anything in a long time."

Thomas reached out and drew the blanket back up, making sure to cover her to the neck. A sheen of sweat pricked his face and arms. He put it down to the heat of the risen sun on the roof close above their heads. He saw the same sweat on Bel's face, the same flush on her cheeks.

"Are you saying Raulf and Lizzie were sweethearts?"

"Not as such, no, but I think Raulf wanted them to be. Trouble is Lizzie's sweet on Osmund Gifforde. She told me that's where they meet, in the copse on Cursneh Hill. It's nice up there. Quiet. Private. You can meet me up there if you want."

"I can think of more romantic spots than where Raulf was killed. Was Osmund Gifforde sweet on Lizzie, too?"

"So she claims."

"What does he say?"

"I don't know what Osmund says because I never asked him."

"Do you think Lizzie will talk to me about Raulf?"

"She's more likely to if I'm with you. We can pretend to be sweethearts. You can even hold my hand." She reached out and took his again.

"When?" Thomas asked.

"Later. Six perhaps, before I go to town for work. Lizzie's house is on the way and her folks will still be out. Do you know where she lives?"

"I do."

"We could climb Cursneh Hill after."

"Let's see what Lizzie says. And you've got to work, haven't you?" He knew she drew ale at The Star Inn while her mother pulled something else in an upstairs room.

"Not if I'm betrothed to Thomas Berrington I don't."

"I think my father might have something to say about that."

"I expect he would. P'raps we'll have to run away to Wales." She let her breath out with a sense of finality. "Time to go now, Tom, before I can't control myself any longer. Six at Sand Pits Lane. Don't be late." With that, Bel rolled onto her side and Thomas rose and left the room.

Adam Brickenden looked up when he passed, stared at him the whole time until Thomas turned the corner of the house. He thought about trying to find Lizzie Martin without Bel, but knew the truth of what she said. It would go better if she was with him. He barely saw the roadway as his feet carried him toward town. The sun was hot, but he no longer felt it. He was trying to work out who might have wanted Raulf Wodall dead, and why. Was it a falling out over a girl? It had happened often enough before and no doubt would happen often enough again, over and over as long as there were men and women and jealousy and lust. Thomas thought a conversation with Osmund Gifforde might prove useful. Bel had distracted him so much he had already stopped worrying what his father might do to him when he returned home.

CHAPTER TEN

Thomas considered returning home but feared his father would know of his escape from the house by now. It would mean another beating, and he'd rather put that off as long as he could. There would be no evading it, but perhaps by evening John Berrington would be in his cups and his aim less true.

The Gifforde farm lay south of the Welsh road, close to Barons' Cross, so he turned away from the roadway and made his way along a rutted track. The Gifforde house was large and badly maintained, the roof sagging in the middle. Thomas's father had offered the opinion it would be easier to knock the whole thing down and start afresh, but his opinions were often harsh and rarely listened to. Least of all by the Giffordes. Thomas wondered how his life would be if his father was less obstinate. Then he thought of all the other fathers he knew and concluded his was no better or worse than any other.

The Gifforde menfolk were turning fresh-cut grass in a field beside the track. Thomas slowed before they saw him and turned aside to make his way to a small copse. The space between the trees was dense with brambles and weeds, and Thomas stayed well away from them. He sheltered in the shade as he watched three men and a boy work the green grass into small stacks. In a few weeks the hay would be dry enough to store in their barn, though whether the barn was watertight enough to make it worthwhile, Thomas doubted.

He glanced at the sun. Almost noon, which meant the men might break to drink ale and take some bread and cheese. He was hoping, as the youngest, they would send Osmund to fetch it. Thomas crouched with his back against the bark of a wizened oak and watched the men as he waited. After a little time his eyes closed and he slipped into a doze.

He woke with a start at the sound of men shouting. At first the sound merged with his dream and it was his father shouting, wanting to know where he had been all night. Then sharp sunlight filled his eyes and Thomas sat up from where he was slumped to see Osmund Gifforde walking round-shouldered in his direction. It was him the shouting had been directed at. Behind him the three remaining men returned to their work.

As Thomas expected, Osmund had been sent home for their midday ration. Watching him, Thomas was puzzled what Lizzie Martin saw in him. Osmund was certainly no catch, though he supposed the Giffordes were well-off enough to offer a girl of little means some surety.

When Osmund was within twenty paces, Thomas rose to his feet and stepped from concealment. Osmund jerked when he saw Thomas and stopped walking. He glanced back at his father and brothers. Thomas waited for him to call out, but he didn't. Instead he started walking again, veering off the direct line to come toward Thomas.

"What are you doing here? Do you want another beating? I can call my brothers if you do. Pa might want to join in this time. He says your father cheated Arthur Wodall on those sheep. Says he cheats everyone." Osmund grinned. "I thought you were meant to hang, Tom. Why aren't you swinging from a rope?"

"Because I didn't kill anyone."

"That's not what folks say."

"What do folks say?"

"That you killed Raulf, what else do you think?"

"The way I hear it, you're more likely to have killed him."

Osmund stopped grinning. "Why would I want to do that?"

"Lizzie Martin," Thomas said.

Osmund firmed his shoulders and tried to stand taller. He was sixteen years old and half a foot taller than Thomas, but he didn't scare him. Thomas knew in a fair fight he had the better of him. The question was if it came to it, would it be a fair fight or not? He glanced at the three strong men still turning hay and decided he could outrun them if need be.

"What about Lizzie?" said Osmund.

"Bel tells me you're sweet on her, but that Raulf was too. Did you fight over her?"

"He follows her around like a calf mooning after a cow, but she don't want anything to do with him. Trouble is her pa thinks I'm not good enough for her and Raulf is." Osmund realised what he'd said and corrected himself. "Was." He shook his head. "Me, a Gifforde, not good enough for a Martin?"

"What did your father think of that?"

"I never told him. I knew he'd lose his temper, same as always, and confront the Martins. I didn't mind anyways.

Lizzie isn't as pretty as she thinks she is. She's no Bel Brickenden. Besides, she wouldn't do nothing, however hard I tried."

Thomas stared at the youth, thinking about Bel's story of Lizzie being attacked the night Raulf died. "How hard did you try?"

"It's a man's duty to press a woman, ain't it? To press on her if he can." Osmund gave a coarse laugh, too loud, and he glanced back at his father and brothers, but it seemed they hadn't heard. "Is that what you been doing with Bel? I thought you'd be too young to get it up, but Bel could get Lazarus hard. She'll be a real treasure to the town soon, just like her Ma. Ask your pa, he'll tell you the same." Osmund shook his head. "That's why you're standing here, ain't it? Because of your pa. The great John Berrington. He won't let his son hang, will he?" Osmund spat at Thomas's feet.

"Where were you the night before last?"

"I was in The Green Man until late."

"Not The Star?"

"We didn't want to go in after we finished with you because your pa and brother were in The Star. Best not to invite trouble. Drank in there last night, too. Arthur Wodall was in The Star, drunk as I he's ever been, I heard. He was sounding off to anyone who'd listen, not that many did. Except for Symon Dawbney's pa. Tell me how you did it, Tom."

"Did what?"

"Kill Raulf. Did he squeal? I wager he did. Pissed himself too, I expect."

"I didn't murder Raulf. Do you think I'd be standing here if anyone in that hearing thought I had?"

"You're John Berrington's son. You could kill us all and nothing would happen to you. Perhaps you'll have to kill

Arthur Wodall before he comes for you, though how you'd manage to do that I don't know. There's not so much of you and Arthur's a hard man. It's another reason I was drinking in The Green Man."

"What time did you leave?"

"What business is it of yours?"

Thomas took a step closer. He believed he could beat Osmund in a fight, and he saw Osmund believed the same thing. He tried to stand his ground, but it was clear he wanted Thomas gone. He glanced toward his father and brothers once more.

"They'll be wondering where their food is. You'll be sorry if they come looking for me and find you here. Do you want another beating, Tom?"

"I'm starting to get used to them. Why did you kill Raulf? Was it a fight over Lizzie?"

"I never killed Raulf. He was more likely to come after me."

"Why?"

"Because I'm the better man, and Lizzie knows it."

Thomas laughed. "Of course you are. Did you know Raulf was with Symon and Walter and they tried to rape Lizzie the night he was killed?"

Osmund stared at Thomas, who saw he knew about the attack. Then Osmund turned and shouted to his father and brothers. Thomas saw them drop their pitchforks and turn at the call.

"Help—Tom Berrington's here! He says he's going to kill me next!" He grinned as if he had gotten one over on Thomas. Which of course he had.

Thomas turned and ran, knowing he was more than fast enough. But he did wonder whether he would have to leave Lemster, at least for a while. His mother's sister lived in

Ludlow and she might let him stay there for a few weeks. Or months. But as his feet flew across the fields, Thomas knew he couldn't run away from his responsibilities. Someone had killed Raulf Wodall, and Thomas was determined to know who and bring them to justice. That or inflict justice himself, if it came to it. He felt as if he had aged years rather than days since his encounter with the boys on the bridge. Something had changed inside him and he didn't know if it was welcome or not, only that he was different. Almost a man.

CHAPTER ELEVEN

As he made his way toward town, Thomas wondered about something Osmund had said—that Arthur Wodall had been sounding off to the Dawbneys. Did that mean only the father, or the son as well? Symon, Walter and Raulf had all been at the river. They had all confronted Thomas. If Thomas hadn't killed Raulf, perhaps Symon or Walter had. Except he couldn't believe it. The three of them were closer than brothers—brothers in mischief, to be sure, but brothers all the same. Far closer than Thomas was to his own brother.

Thomas wanted someone to talk matters over with and could think of only one person that might humour him. He followed the unnamed alleys south of the market square, not wanting to run into either Symon or Walter, and entered the Priory grounds through a small gate in the wall. Brother Bernard wasn't there, one of the monks informed him when asked. He had gone foraging for herbs. Thomas had accompanied him on several occasions and knew there were only four or five places he could be. He found him at the second of them.

The Marsh stood north of the town in the damp fields bounded on one side by the Lugge and on the other by the Kenwater. Patches of reeds grew tall in places and Brother Bernard was kneeling behind one as he picked at something on the ground. Thomas tried to approach silently, but was still a dozen paces away when Brother Bernard said, "You make more noise than a skittish cow, Tom." He put whatever he had found into a leather satchel hanging around his neck and stood.

"Can I help?" Thomas asked.

"You can if you know what St John's Wort looks like."

"Everyone knows that." Thomas looked around. "There's a patch there ... another over there."

"You're both right and wrong, Tom. It is true those are what you seek, but not many would recognise them. Even fewer would know of its uses. Do you remember them?"

"A tea made from it aids the afflicted of the mind, and the oil is good for applying to wounds. It can stop them going bad."

Brother Bernard smiled. "It looks like you could do with some of that on those bruises of yours, though a paste of Arnica would be better for them." Brother Bernard came closer and put a finger under Thomas's chin. He turned his head one way then the other. "Can you see all right through that eye?"

"I think so." Thomas closed the other and looked around through the one that had been swollen. He nodded. "I see fine."

"No black dots floating about?"

Thomas shook his head.

"Good. I have seen men lose their sight if that happens after a blow. They beat you good, didn't they? Who was it?"

"Does it matter?"

"No, I expect not, I was merely curious is all. The bruises are healing well. They do in the young." Brother Bernard started toward the clump of St John's Wort and Thomas fell in beside him, aware of the man's height and easy strength. Envious of them, knowing they were things he might aspire to but never attain. Not unless he too went to fight the heathens in Spain, but probably not even then.

"It was the Giffordes did it, mostly," Thomas said. "Though Symon and Raulf both wanted a piece of me too. It was the night Raulf was killed."

"It would have to be, wouldn't it? You didn't kill him, did you, Tom?"

Thomas stopped, waiting for Brother Bernard to do the same and turn to him.

"Do you think I could?"

"You're not big, but you're strong and fast, so yes I think you could. That's not the same as saying I think you did. Good fighter you might be, but there's no bad in you. Do you think I don't see that, boy?"

Thomas didn't like being called boy. Not today. Not after he had been so sorely tempted by Bel Brickenden. That would not have been the action of a boy, would it? Perhaps best not to make mention of any of that to Brother Bernard, he thought.

"You used to be a good fighter, didn't you?"

"In another life, but I have put all such things behind me now."

"I thought you could teach me how to fight better," Thomas said. "How not to get beaten so bad the next time."

"The best thing you need to learn, when there is a next time as there surely will be, is how to walk away, how to distract them from starting a fight."

"Can't always do that, can you."

"No, not always, but it's worth a try first." Brother Bernard smiled. "And then you hit them hard and hit them fast. Start with the biggest, or the one with a weapon."

"Are you sure you didn't see the fight?"

Brother Bernard only smiled again and started walking. "What is it you want to talk to me about, Tom?"

"I need to tell somebody what I think and you're the only one I know of who won't tell me to go away."

"I might do that if you talk nonsense."

They reached the patch of St John's Wort and Brother Bernard waited to see if Thomas knew which parts were needed. Which he did.

"No you won't. Do you think I don't know you either, Bernard?"

Brother Bernard flicked a finger at Thomas, but it came nowhere near landing. "Go on then, regale me with your theories. It will help pass the time if nothing else."

"I don't have theories, only a tangle of thoughts that I need help to tease out. Raulf was stabbed, and when he fought me, Roger Gifforde had a knife, but I don't think he killed him."

"Why not? And most men carry a knife, don't they?"

"Roger had no quarrel with Raulf. You showed me the body, remember. Whoever killed Raulf was angry. All those blows. That wasn't an execution, it was done in a rage. Maybe whoever did it never meant to actually kill him, but—"

"You don't use a knife on someone unless you mean to kill them."

"I suppose not. So whoever it was did it struck him in anger, or because they wanted Raulf dead."

"Why?"

"Why what?"

"Who would want Raulf dead, and for what reason? Do you know the reasons, Tom? Envy, greed, love, lust, disgust and religion."

Thomas was surprised Brother Bernard included religion considering his chosen profession, but couldn't disagree with him. Much blood had been shed over religion, he knew, and no doubt much more remained to be spilled. Perhaps forever.

"So which is it?" he asked.

"How am I meant to know that? That's enough of the Wort, now. Put it in the sack with the rest of the herbs. Now, I need mushrooms. The red kind with white spots. Where will I find them?"

"Plenty of those in Eaton Woods, pretty much anywhere you get pine and birch growing close together. I can show you if you want, it's on my way home."

"Are you going home?"

"I'm not doing much good in town, though I'm going to talk to Lizzie Martin later, with Bel."

"Why?"

"You know Lizzie was attacked the night Raulf was killed. Didn't you see the scratches on Bel's legs when she came and spoke for me?"

"I try not to look at Bel Brickenden's legs if I can help it. I'll let you do all the looking for me. I assume when you say Lizzie was attacked, someone wanted something specific?"

"You know what they wanted."

"Lizzie's a pretty girl. Men will want her, of course they will."

Thomas smiled. "I thought you weren't meant to look."

"I'm a monk, Tom, not blind or dead. Lizzie's pretty, but not as pretty as Bel. Or her mother."

"Except anyone can have Joan Brickenden for a penny,

and I don't suppose it will be so long until they can have Bel as well." Thomas sighed at the thought, disturbed by it.

"A penny, is it?"

When Thomas looked at Brother Bernard, he saw he was smiling. "I don't know if her being attacked has anything to do with what happened to Raulf, but I still want to talk to her. I don't know what's important or not until I've found out as much as I can."

They reached the Ludlow road and used it to reach the stone bridge across the Lugge before striking off toward thick woodland that coated the western flank of Eaton Hill. A half mile to the right, Thomas could see his house. A curl of smoke rising from the chimney told him his mother had lit the stove in the kitchen. Thomas felt a strong urge to turn aside and head there. His mother would welcome him, and he could play with little Angnes and try to make her laugh. Let someone else solve the mystery of who killed Raulf. Someone better suited to the job. Except Thomas knew if he didn't do it, nobody would. Nobody cared except Raulf's family, and he knew they wouldn't pursue the matter any further. As far as they were concerned, Thomas was guilty and, even if he was not, he would do as well as anyone else.

Thinking of the Wodalls brought Susan to mind. Pretty Susan Wodall, who had set her sights on Thomas at one time. Though no doubt those sights would now be set on someone else. Even so, he knew she might know something. Raulf might have talked to her, let something slip, and Thomas knew he would have to question her. But not now, and not later today either. There was too much else to do, including showing Brother Bernard where the red mushrooms grew. After he had done that, there would be no time to return home. Already the afternoon was softening into a long evening, and Thomas had to meet Bel Brickenden and talk to Lizzie Martin. The thought of both girls settled an unease through him. He felt a tension running across his skin that made him want to scratch an itch he couldn't locate.

CHAPTER TWELVE

By the time Thomas reached Sand Pit Lane, Bel was sitting on a low wall swinging her legs. She had raised her skirts above her knees so her pale legs showed.

"Do the scratches hurt?" Thomas asked as he pulled himself onto the wall beside her.

"They itch a bit, but don't hurt, no."

"I could probably make a salve up for them if you want. Brother Bernard showed me how, and I think I can remember it."

Bel smiled and nudged him with her shoulder. "You can come and put it on me yourself later if you like. I'm sure I've got scratches elsewhere, too."

Thomas laughed, eased by Bel's reliable teasing.

"How much would you charge for this salve of yours?" she asked.

"It would be free for you, you know it would."

"Then you can definitely come and see me."

Thomas dropped down from the wall and offered his hands to lift Bel down. When he put them around her waist, his fingers almost met behind her back, so slim was she.

"We'd better go and talk to Lizzie before I do something stupid."

"Wouldn't be stupid, Tom, you know it wouldn't. But you're right, we should talk to Lizzie before her folks get home from work."

They found Lizzie Martin sitting in her back garden on a wooden bench, eyes closed and face turned up to the lowering sun. Bel put a finger to her lips and crept up on her, grabbed Lizzie's shoulders and shouted in her ear. Lizzie shot to her feet, hands up to defend herself.

Thomas saw Bel regretted her attempt to tease in an instant, no doubt aware of the memories being grabbed had brought back. She embraced the girl, speaking soft words to her. Lizzie looked at Thomas over Bel's shoulder, her face lacking any expression, as if something had been rubbed out in her soul. Bel broke the embrace and waved Thomas over as Lizzie retook her seat. Bel sat beside her. There was no room for Thomas so he knelt facing the bench. He didn't want to stand towering over them.

"Tom wants to know what happened the night Raulf died."

Lizzie's eyes found something fascinating in the hedgerow and wouldn't meet Thomas's.

Bel took Lizzie's hand in hers. "You can tell Tom anything, you know you can. He's not like the other boys. Sometimes I think he's ten times older than his years."

Thomas suppressed a laugh. Bel's statement would give him 130 years and he'd be long dead.

"All boys are the same," Lizzie said, no emotion in her voice.

"I told you, Tom's different. If it had been Tom come along that night, he'd have beaten them all soundly."

"It would be him got the beating with the three of them,

just like he did in the market square that night. Symon's big and he's strong."

"Symon Dawbney was one of them, was he?" Thomas said.

Lizzie's eyes finally met his and he saw her shoulders lose some of their tension. He studied her face. She was almost as pretty as Bel, but there was a lack of something that lessened her beauty. Perhaps that inner light Bel possessed.

"Bel told you who they were, did she?" Lizzie glanced at her friend as if in disappointment at the telling of a secret.

"Bel wouldn't tell me anything. She said it was your place to do that, but only if you wanted to. Do you want to, Lizzie?"

She lifted one shoulder in a quick shrug. "I expect you know who they are. Same troublemakers who were after you."

"Except they wanted something else from you, didn't they?" It felt strange to Thomas to be talking of such adult matters with Lizzie, who was two years older than him. Perhaps Bel was right and he did carry an older soul inside himself, but if he did, he had no idea where it was, or what good it might do him.

"You're a boy, Tom, you know what they wanted."

"Why?"

"Don't you think I'm pretty enough to be wanted?"

"Of course you are, you're more than pretty enough for any boy to set his sights on, but that's not what this was about, is it?"

"I already said you know what they wanted."

"And I asked you why, on that night, they came after you. Where was this exactly? A patch of briars, I know that much, but there are briars everywhere."

"I was planning on going up Cursneh Hill," said Lizzie.

"Who with?"

"Nobody." Her eyes skittered away to the side again. "I like to sit up there and watch the sun go down."

"I heard tell Raulf went up there sometimes with you. Is that right?"

"We walked out for a while, everyone knows we did, but I told him I didn't want to be with him anymore. Not unless he gave up those friends of his. Symon and Walter. Symon's a bully and Walter's sly. Raulf was better than both of them put together. Not as nice as you, Tom, but nice enough when he was on his own. Used to be, anyway."

"So he wasn't with you that night?"

Lizzie shook her head. "Not on the hill, no."

"Who was?"

Lizzie looked away. Bel continued to hold her hand, silent, supportive. Her eyes met Thomas's and she offered a tiny nod, but whether in encouragement or approval he couldn't tell. He wished he was older and wiser, but knew that wishing wouldn't make it true. He would have to cope as well as he could.

"You were with someone, weren't you?" Thomas wanted to see if Lizzie would offer Osmund Gifforde's name.

"Doesn't matter if I was or not. Those boys attacked me before I went up the hill." She shook her head, perhaps trying to shake the remembrance from it, but if so, it didn't work that way. "I was sore afraid, Tom." Her eyes met his, her own showing tears now. "I knew what they wanted so I tried to fight them, but there were three of them and that Symon Dawbney's as big as a man." She gave a tight laugh. "Well, some of him is."

"Some of him?"

"I told you what they wanted, and he wanted it most of

all. He pulled his hose down and his thing was sticking out. Big boy he might be, but he's not so big down there."

Thomas suppressed a smile. He glanced at Bel, who raised an eyebrow. "You've seen so many boys you can compare?"

"Don't need to've done, do I? It was small, but he'd have still hurt me if he'd tried to ... well, you know what."

"What were the others doing while Symon was waving his manhood in the wind? I assume the other two were Walter and Raulf?"

"They were holding me down. Symon said he was going to be first, but they could both take their turn when he was done." The tears in her eyes brimmed over and ran down her cheeks, but she made no move to wipe them away. "I thought Raulf wouldn't do anything until I saw how he looked at me. We were sweet on each other not so long ago, but I saw he wanted to hurt me as much as Symon. I think he wanted to hurt me even more than the others."

"Did Symon..." Thomas didn't want to finish the thought, didn't suppose he needed to.

"He'd lifted my skirts, but then Bel came along and she heard us. They were making such a mess of noise. She came into the briars and slapped Symon around the head so hard, I thought she might have knocked his brains loose if he had any. Then she looked at his thing and laughed. Told him her ma would only charge a farthing for something that size and he'd be better off going to The Star. I thought he was going to hit her when she said that."

Thomas looked toward Bel. "Is this the truth?"

She nodded, suppressing a smile. "Including the farthing."

"I don't understand," Thomas said. "There were three of

101

them. Symon is as strong as an ox, and Walter and Raulf aren't weaklings. Why did they leave you both alone?"

"Because I am Bel Brickenden and they knew what would happen if they so much as laid a finger on me. My ma has serviced all their fathers, most of their brothers too, same as she has your father and brother, Tom, you know she has. She's the best whore in town and the three of them knew a heap of trouble would come down on them if they so much as touched me. And because Lizzie was with me, they knew they couldn't touch a hair on her head either." Bel lifted Lizzie's hand and kissed the back of it before returning it to her lap.

Thomas recognised the truth of her words, but he didn't like to think of Bel's mother servicing any of those men. Joan Brickenden was kind and pretty, and she always seemed somehow innocent to him. He never thought of her as a whore, despite Bel teasing him about that cursed penny.

"Who were you with on Cursneh Hill, Lizzie?" Thomas asked, and something in his voice made her gaze meet his.

"It don't matter."

"You know it does. Suppose he witnessed the attack on you, or heard about it from someone? What if he wanted to take revenge on the boys who attacked his girl?"

Lizzie shook her head. "He wouldn't do that."

"Then there's no harm if you tell me who he is."

"Tell him, Lizzie," said Bel. "Tell Tom who you were with."

"I can't. If I tell him, Tom will go and ask questions and it will get out the two of us were together on the hill." Lizzie rose to her feet, snatching her hand from inside Bel's. "I can't tell him!" She turned and walked fast toward the back door of the house.

Thomas was faster. He caught her in the porch and

turned her around, taller by half a foot, his hands firm on her shoulders. He felt the tremble in them and knew he was acting like those three boys, but he needed her to admit the truth to him. He stepped closer so his chest pressed against her, pushed her back against the door.

"I know who you were with, Lizzie, but I want you to tell me."

"Are you going to hurt me, Tom? Or more? I don't suppose Bel is going to save me from you, is she?"

"Depends on whether you tell me the truth or not."

"I told you, I can't!"

Thomas pushed harder against her, unsettled at the feelings the contact raised in him, disgusted at his own reaction, but he had gone too far to back down now. Then he saw a change in Lizzie's eyes and knew he had won.

"Osmund Gifforde," she said, the tension leaving her body.

"Did Raulf know about you and Osmund?"

"Nobody knew, Tom. Do you think we are stupid? Nobody knew."

Thomas released her and stepped away. Lizzie fumbled with the latch of the door, opened it and disappeared inside. When Thomas turned, he found Bel inches away from him, her eyes bright and looking up into his.

"I knew you wouldn't hurt her. Do you think Osmund killed Raulf?"

"I spoke to him only a little after noon today and if I had to swear on it, I'd say not. He admitted to me he's been seeing Lizzie, but swore me to keep it to myself."

Bel laughed. "I'm sure he did. The Giffordes are well thought of in Lemster, and Lizzie's folks don't even own this house. Her mother serves ale in The Green Man and her father finds whatever work he can. Lizzie knows nothing can ever come of anything between her and Osmund, however pretty she might be."

"I wonder if Osmund thinks the same way," Thomas said.

Bel reached out and took his hand. "Sometimes love doesn't do much thinking, Tom, it just is. Are you going to talk to Osmund again tonight?"

"I don't know. I expect not. I want to think about what Lizzie told me, think about what else I've learned. I wonder if Raulf knew Lizzie was sweet on Osmund?"

"I don't know, but you know who might, don't you?"

He did, but was reluctant to talk to that person. Susan Wodall had been more or less promised to him in marriage when they were of an age, and that age was not so far in the future in these parts. She was a year older than Thomas and thought herself clever and cultured, and perhaps she was. Now, no doubt, she blamed him for the death of her brother.

"I'm not going to The Star tonight," said Bel, the statement coming out of the blue.

"Why are you telling me? Do you want to come with me to see Susan?"

Bel shook her head. "I'm going home. You can come and visit me later if you want. You know where I'll be."

Thomas did, but he could make no promise. He had more work to do, and thoughts of Bel Brickenden would only distract him. As he walked back in the direction of the town, he wondered if this was how someone like Brother Bernard felt all the time, surrounded by temptation on all sides but determined to resist it. Thomas didn't think he could ever be that strong. Already he wanted to turn around and walk with Bel back to her house. Back to the warm room above her father's workshop.

CHAPTER THIRTEEN

Several hours of daylight remained as Thomas skirted the town and headed toward the Wodall farm. Heavy thunder-clouds had gathered in the west, preceded by a warm wind that promised rain before nightfall. Still reluctant to think about returning home, Thomas knew he would get wet, but he judged the rain was an hour away yet as he followed the rutted lane toward the farmhouse where he hoped to find Susan Wodall.

The Wodalls weren't as elevated as John Berrington, but they were still important people in Lemster. Some time over the last year, they and his father had clearly had a conversation. Susan was a girl of fourteen years and would shortly be in need of a marriage—or at the least the promise of one. Thomas was considered a catch. Or he would be once he settled down and stopped showing an interest in things he shouldn't. Thomas hoped that would never happen. He had heard all of this from his father one evening as they sat around the fireplace, his mother with them, as well as his brother John. Only little Angnes was missing, asleep in her cot in his parents' bedroom. No doubt talk of marriage meant little to her. It meant little to Thomas, other than it was made plain a match between the Wodalls and the Berringtons was considered a good thing. By his father, at least. When Thomas glanced at his mother, her mouth was a tight line, as if holding in any words that might try to escape. It was not an unusual expression, one Thomas had seen often enough before to know what it meant.

Thomas's own wishes were not even asked for. A deal had been struck.

And now that deal, that promise, was tossed to the four winds. Or were the Wodalls greedy enough to still want a marriage even if they believed Thomas had murdered their son? As Thomas walked toward the fine wooden barn set across the yard from the house, he couldn't believe any father or mother would be that forgiving. Which is why he didn't approach the house directly.

The interior of the barn was warm after the day's heat and carried the sweet scent of dry hay. It was piled in one corner and almost filled the upper platform, which was where Thomas climbed to. He settled down on a stack of hay to wait, knowing at some point Susan would be sent out for firewood. He had noted the lack of smoke from the chimney as he approached, which meant a fire had not yet been lit. A fresh stack of logs was piled next to the hay, more uncut wood scattered across the dirt floor waiting for tomorrow's axe.

Thomas thought about what Lizzie Martin had told him, about her and Osmund Gifforde. Had Raulf found out about their liaison and confronted Osmund? Thomas thought not. Raulf was no coward, but he wasn't stupid either. Osmund was three year the older and stronger by far. Raulf would swallow his pride and look for someone else. Just as the Wodalls had set their sights on a marriage between their daughter and Thomas, so many families in Lemster would welcome a match with Raulf. Well, they would have when he was alive. Now there would be other plans being made. Thomas wondered if Bel had heard any rumours, though it was still early days. In the weeks and months to come, relationships would shift and be reappraised.

The sound of a closing door brought Thomas back to the present and he knelt close to the top of the ladder. Susan Wodall entered carrying an empty basket woven from rushes. Thomas watched her, judging what he had lost. Susan was pretty enough, tall and shapely, but she carried a sense of entitlement that reduced her attraction, for Thomas at least, though he suspected some might find it beguiling. She was dressed more plainly than he had seen her before, when their meetings had been highly arranged and chaperoned. Now she wore a white linen blouse and dark skirt, her feet pushed into wooden clogs that slapped against her heels with each step.

Thomas waited until Susan bent to fill the basket, and then, as she started to lift it, he slid down the ladder and ran across the barn. Susan spun around, a look of fear on her face. She dropped the basket and raised her hands as if to fend off an attack. When she saw who it was, her fear turned to instant rage. She struck out as Thomas came close, slapping him hard across the cheek, and he felt her nails scratch into his skin. He grabbed her around the waist and lifted her from her feet, surprised at how light she was, and tossed her onto the hay pile. When she opened her mouth to scream, he straddled her and put a hand over her mouth.

"I didn't kill him," Thomas said, feeling Susan writhe beneath him. Despite her slightness, she was strong, and

Thomas had to grip her tight between his knees to stop himself being thrown off.

Susan mumbled something beneath his hand and her fists punched at him. Thomas had only the one hand to fend them off so took the blows as his due.

"I'll remove my hand if you stop hitting me and promise not to scream."

She glared at him, dark eyes filled with venom, but she stopped writhing and stopped hitting him. Thomas relaxed the pressure of his hand over her mouth, then drew it away, waiting, ready to put it back if she called out. But Susan lay there, passive now, as if all the fight had gone from her.

"What do you want with me?" she demanded.

"To talk, nothing more."

"Why did you kill Raulf?" Susan's eyes changed, the hate fading to be replaced by tears, and Thomas saw she had loved her brother. It came as a surprise to him.

"I didn't kill him. Someone else did."

"So you say, but I hear the Earl's man has other ideas." She gave a tight smile. "We are all coming to watch you kick when they string you up, Tom, and I'll be laughing when they do."

That was the trouble with an arrangement between families, he and Susan had never had the time or privacy to form any kind of relationship. He had never kissed her, never even touched her hand. Until now, he thought. He grew aware of her strong litheness beneath him, of the thinness of linen separating them. He became uncomfortable at a sense of arousal that grew as he straddled her, and felt disgust even as the arousal became stronger. He saw Susan was aware of it as well, but instead of showing disgust, she smiled. She knew she had power of him, as women often had power over men who were but weak creatures driven by their lusts.

"Did you know Raulf was sweet on Lizzie Martin?"

Susan tried to sit up and Thomas grasped her wrists. He pushed her back down, his face half a foot from hers. She thrust up as if trying to throw him off, but he was too heavy, despite being a year the younger. He watched a resignation fill Susan's eyes and he released her wrists. She rubbed at them as if they were sore, but Thomas knew he had been gentle with her.

"He said he was seeing someone but wouldn't tell me who. Now I know why. Father would have thrashed him if he knew he was walking out with Lizzie Martin."

"Do you think your father might have found out?"

"He might have thrashed Raulf, but he wouldn't kill him. What do you think my family are? It's your father who rides to war alongside the Earl, not mine. Perhaps he killed Raulf."

"Don't be stupid. Why would my father want to kill him?"

"Same reason as you did."

"I told you, I didn't kill him."

"I don't believe you, and neither do Mother or Father. They are already talking of finding a new match for me. The Giffordes have been mentioned, but Mother would prefer someone of higher standing. I think she dreams of a liaison with Henry Talbot."

"Who is illegitimate," Thomas said.

"But still the fruit of John Talbot's loins."

"Did Raulf tell you where he was going the night he was killed?"

"Why would he ever do such a thing?"

"Did you know he used to meet Lizzie up on Cursneh Hill?"

"We talked, of course, but never about that kind of thing. He did ask me about you once and I told him you were a gentleman. That was before you killed him, of course. You're not such a gentleman now, are you, Tom?" She gave a sly smile and Thomas knew she was aware of his arousal. He had hoped it might fade, but the hope had been in vain. He was beginning to understand how men were oftentimes brutal with women. His blood sang hot in his veins and it would be easy to tip over into taking what he wanted. If he wasn't Thomas Berrington. At least he hoped that was true. Disgusted with himself, he released his hold on Susan and stood.

"You can go, take your firewood indoors. You're no use to me if you don't know anything."

Susan continued to sprawl on the hay pile for a moment, staring up at him, and then her eyes flickered to one side and Thomas leapt the other way as the heavy metal head of an axe scythed through the air where his head had been only the moment before.

Arthur Wodall stood with feet spread, the axe held firm in his grip, his face bright red with rage.

Thomas held his hands up, only as he did so recognising how stupid the move was. One swing and he could lose one or both of them.

"I didn't kill Raulf," he said.

Arthur Wodall only shook his head and took a step closer. "Nobody else has been arrested, have they? You did it, Tom, I know you did. Now take your punishment like a man and I'll make it quick for you."

"Kill me and it'll be you who hangs."

"Not for a justified killing I won't." He took another step.

As Arthur Wodall raised the axe, Thomas took his chance and threw himself under the descending blade. He knocked the man off his feet with the force of their meeting. Thomas skipped over the man's prostrate body and sprinted through the door of the barn. He kept going until the bellows from behind faded, and then he kept going a little more. When he finally slowed, he found himself skirting the base of Cursneh Hill with the thunder clouds now almost on top of the town. The first fat drops of rain splashed on the dry roadway, and then the heavens opened, soaking Thomas in an instant. Had the rain been cold, it might have changed everything, but Thomas's blood still sang with his power over Susan and his escape from her father. And Bel's promise rang in his mind.

"You can come visit me later if you want," she had said. "You know where I'll be."

And he did.

CHAPTER FOURTEEN

Thomas woke sweating and confused, not knowing where he was, only that he was not lying in his own bed. He opened his eyes to a bright ray of sunlight falling directly on him and closed them again.

"You're awake," said an amused female voice next to him.

All at once, memory returned, and with it shame. He rolled his head to one side and opened his eyes again to see the pretty, amused face of Bel Brickenden. She reached her hand out and laid it against his chest.

Bel laughed. "Have you changed your mind yet?"

The question reminded him of what Bel had offered the night before, an offer he had been too scared to accept.

"If I thought you meant what you said, I might."

"I do mean it. You're tall and you're strong and you have a position in this town." Bel laughed again at the expression she saw on his face. "It's all right, Tom, I don't want you to marry me. At least, I don't expect you to offer."

He thought about what it might be like to be married to Bel Brickenden, the prettiest girl in Lemster.

"Whatever it is you want, you can have it," Thomas said, and at that moment he meant it.

"You know what I want, Tom."

And he did. At least, he thought he did. He wanted it too. Him and Bel living together. Except he knew his father would never allow such a thing.

* * *

The room was even warmer an hour later. Bel lay curled beneath his arm. They had spent the time profitably, with Bel teaching him the right way to kiss a girl, and Thomas finally believed he was starting to get the hang of it.

"Did you go to see Susan Wodall after you left me last night?" Bel asked.

"I did."

"I should be annoyed you were thinking about someone else, but I forgive you." She kissed his shoulder, a chaste kiss this time.

"I wasn't thinking of Susan. I was only thinking of you." Thomas felt an unease, a turning point. He wondered exactly what Bel wanted from him. What he wanted from her. He felt drained of all need, lying next to her, and he thought he could easily get used to her presence.

He heard his father's voice in his head.

She's a whore's daughter, Tom, and she'll be a whore herself soon enough, mark my words. Use her if you want, but that's all. You're a Berrington, destined for better than Bel Brickenden.

Thomas wasn't so sure. He couldn't imagine anyone prettier or sweeter than Bel.

"I know I'm too young," he said.

"That's not true, Tom."

"Not for what we did, maybe, but for other things I am."

"What other things are there?"

"I have expectations on me," he said. "Everyone expects

something from me, though I'm a second son so there's less pressure, I admit. It's John who will inherit. John who will garner titles. Maybe I'll be allowed to follow my heart."

Bel lifted up so she could stare into his eyes. "My, you've gone all serious. Do I need to kiss you again?"

He smiled and shook his head. He knew he couldn't tell Bel what was really on his mind. Not now, perhaps never.

"Not yet. I want to talk about yesterday."

"Yesterday or last night?"

"Yesterday."

"What about yesterday do you want to talk about?"

"The things I found out." When he felt Bel shift, he added, "The things we found out."

"Tell me what you found out, Tom. Are you thirsty?"

He nodded, and Bel slipped from beneath the blanket and padded to where a pitcher and cup sat on a low bench, clearly used as a table. She filled the cup and brought it back, handed it to him, then once more lay down beside him. Thomas drank, then passed the cup to Bel who did the same. She wiped her mouth and curled against him.

"It was mostly what Lizzie said, but some of what Susan told me as well."

Bel said nothing, and he turned his head, wondering if she had drifted into sleep, but she was staring at him, waiting. Thomas felt a weight of responsibility. He might only have thirteen years, but this girl trusted him, listened to him. Responsibility and hope. Perhaps he could have what he wanted after all.

"What's funny, Tom?" asked Bel, and he knew he must have been smiling.

"I was thinking, that's all."

Bel tapped his forehead with a knuckle. "Thinking's

overrated. Thinking can make a man do the wrong thing, come to the wrong conclusion. You think a lot, don't you?"

"Do I?"

"I know you do, and it's why I like you. You're not like the other boys and men."

"Brother Bernard thinks, too," Thomas said.

Bel laughed. "I don't know Brother Bernard like I know you, but I'll take your word for it. You and Brother Bernard, then. No doubt you both think more than is good for you."

Bel had distracted him from his thoughts. So much for thinking. He shifted on the bed, trying to get comfortable, and Bel moved against him and he almost became distracted all over again.

"The way I see it," he said, "is there are three people who might have killed Raulf."

"I think I know who, but tell me anyway."

Thomas rolled his head and kissed the tip of her nose. "I l—like you, Bel."

She smiled and repeated his hesitation. "I l—like you too, Tom Berrington."

He saw she knew what he had almost said and didn't care. Maybe he wanted them to say it to each other, despite his youth and the expectations on him.

"The first ones to think about are Symon and Walter, and then I want to talk about Osmund Gifforde."

"Because he was sweet on Lizzie?"

Thomas nodded. Bel was clever. It came as more of a comfort than a surprise.

"Symon and Walter were with Raulf when they attacked Lizzie." He stared at the pattern of sunlight coming through the gaps in the wooden walls. From downstairs he heard Bel's father moving around and wondered what he would say if he came upstairs and found them lying together.

Perhaps nothing. Thomas Berrington would be considered a catch for a brick-maker's daughter.

"She said Raulf was angry," said Bel. "Symon was riled, so was Walter, but Raulf was angry. She was more scared of him than the others."

"Which is the stronger, Bel? Anger or lust?"

She laughed. "Well, come right out and say what's on your mind, Tom. I expect you think I'm a girl who knows the answer to that, do you?"

"I didn't mean it that way."

"I know you didn't, so it's all right. It's a good question, though. One I should be an expert in considering what Ma's job is. I know a great deal about lust, but less about anger. I expect you know more about that than me."

"I'm not angry."

"I know you're not, but your father is, and so is your brother. Your mother is sweet, and I suspect your little sister will be too. But you know about anger from your menfolk, don't you?"

Thomas nodded. "I expect so, yes."

"The anger missed you, didn't it?"

"I hope so."

"So do I."

Thomas glanced at her, looked away, not yet willing to open his heart to her even though he suspected he knew what Bel's answer would be if he did. He might have no ambition for himself, but he was the son of John Berrington, an important man in these parts. Was that why Bel liked him? And then the thought came—did Bel like him, or did she see him as nothing more than a means to better herself? Thomas wished he was older and wiser and knew women better than he did. Or even knew them at all.

"Yes, I know anger," he said, knowing he had to stick to

the matter at hand to stop his mind drifting to more pleasurable thoughts. Those might come again later, but today he wanted to find Raulf's killer. The thought of today made him aware that Peter Markel might have already returned to continue his interrogation.

Bel stroked his neck and shoulders. "What's wrong, Tom?"

"They might hang me today."

"No they won't. You didn't do anything."

"When does that ever matter? Innocent men are hanged all the time. The Wodalls want to see someone dangle for the death of Raulf and they see me as that person."

"You're John Berrington's son, Tom. The Wodalls are important around here, but John Berrington works for John Talbot, and he's the law in these parts. Even if you had killed Raulf, you would walk free."

"I didn't kill him."

"I know you didn't, so tell me who did."

"Osmund," Thomas said, the word coming as more of a surprise to him than Bel. "Osmund Gifforde killed Raulf, and I think Lizzie Martin knows he did it. Of course..."

Bel sat up. "Of course what?"

"Raulf used to walk out with Lizzie."

Bel snorted. "Walked out? Or more?"

"With Lizzie Martin?" Thomas couldn't believe anything more than the holding of hands, perhaps a chaste touching of lips, no more.

"Raulf's a toucher," Bel said, as if she knew.

"And Osmund?"

"All men are touchers, Tom, even you. But I don't mind it when you do it." She grinned. "Don't mind it at all."

Thomas felt a flash of undeserved jealousy. "And the others?"

Bel shrugged.

"All right, whatever you say, Raulf was a toucher and Lizzie isn't the sweet innocent I thought she was." He saw Bel nod and he smiled, but the smile faded as he painted a picture in his mind. "I wonder if Raulf took the other two with him?"

"You're thinking too fast for me now," said Bel. "You need to explain."

"Raulf was hurt when Lizzie said she didn't want to see him anymore. Raulf never was strong that way. Sometimes it seemed he wanted to be hurt so he could revel in it. It's why he made such a fuss when I tossed him into the Lugge. He was a cry-baby, but that doesn't matter. What does matter is Raulf was hurt. He wanted to hurt someone in return, but he was not strong enough on his own, so he took Symon and Walter with him up Cursneh Hill. They probably spied on Osmund and Lizzie for a while. I believe that's why when the two of them parted, the boys followed Lizzie and attacked her."

"Why her? If it was me, I'd wait until they separated and go after Osmund. It was him who stole Lizzie from Raulf."

"Raulf was with Symon and Walter when they attacked Lizzie, but he was found the following morning on top of Cursneh Hill. I have no idea what he was doing up there, unless he thought Osmund hadn't come down, but one way or another I believe he must have confronted him, not aware Osmund still had his brother's knife."

Bel sat up again. "What?" She slapped his belly. "Make sense, Tom—*what* knife?"

"When the Giffordes beat me, Roger had a knife, but he dropped it. I saw Osmund pick it up and slip it inside his boot. When Raulf confronted him, the knife must have come out and Osmund killed Raulf. What I don't know is whether Symon and Walter were there as well." Thomas rose from the bed. "I have to go and tell Peter Markel how it all happened. And then..." he found his shirt and pulled it on, but could only find one boot, "...and then Osmund knew he had to implicate someone else so he came looking for me and hit me. I expect he even planted the knife on me somewhere, but he didn't reckon on the Lugge stealing it away. I was meant to drown. He threw me in the river with the intention of drowning me, but I didn't. A felled tree saved my life, Bel, and here I am." Thomas shook his head. "I have no idea why he didn't call out to his folks sooner when I questioned him yesterday. Though he did in the end. He's afraid I'll work out the truth and it will be him who hangs."

"If what you claim is true, he may not." Bel got to her feet. She found his lost boot under the bed and threw it at him. "If it happened like you say and Raulf attacked Osmund, he can claim self-defence. Neither family is important enough to have a charge set aside, unlike you."

"I need to find Symon and Walter," Thomas said. "They might have witnessed everything. And if not, they can at least tell me when Raulf left them." He stared at Bel. "What if he was already dead when the Giffordes came to beat me, and they knew it? Peter Markel released me and they wanted me dead to protect Osmund. I have to confront Lizzie again and tell her I know the truth."

"In that case, I'd better come with you."

CHAPTER FIFTEEN

As they entered town, Thomas saw Symon Dawbney and Walter Gifforde sitting together on the mile marker that read Ludlow 11, Hereford 12, one name atop the other. Something in his step must have messaged his intent because Bel grasped his hand.

"No, Tom," she said, tugging at him.

"I'm not afraid of them."

"Maybe not, but you should be. Symon's twice your size, and Walter's always ready to join in with mischief."

"I told you, I'm not afraid of them." Thomas snatched his hand from Bel's grip and walked toward the pair.

It was Walter saw him first, and he started before recovering himself and leaning in to say something to Symon, who lifted his gaze. He grinned.

"I want to talk to you," Thomas said, coming to a halt four feet from them. Close enough, he judged, to message some measure of threat, far enough to respond if they attacked.

"Well here we are, talk all you want."

Thomas held a finger up. "First—what did you think you were doing with Lizzie Martin two nights ago?"

Symon looked past Thomas to where Bel hung back and laughed. "What do you think we were doing? Only what she wanted. Only what she deserved. Just like that one there. Are you and Bel sweet on each other now, Tom? Well get in the line for her. Every man and boy in this town plans on tupping her as soon as she decides to follow her ma into the family business."

Thomas held a second finger up, hoping the pair of them could count to more than one. "Second—when did Raulf leave you the night he died? I know you were all three of you together, so when was it?"

Walter frowned and looked toward Symon, though of the two of them, he was the only one with sense enough to answer. That or come up with a believable lie.

"Raulf was with us all night," said Symon, getting his response in first.

"Clearly he wasn't if he was found dead on Cursneh Hill at sunrise."

"What he meant was Raulf went home the same time we did," said Walter.

"Which was?" Thomas asked.

"After you was beaten." The grin returned to Symon's dull face. "It was a fine show, that was."

"Obviously after the fight," Thomas said, "because Raulf was there. I saw him."

"Did it hurt?" said Walter.

"Of course it hurt, but sometimes you have to take what's coming. What did you do after the fight?"

"We don't need to answer your questions," said Symon, and Walter nodded agreement.

"I know you attacked Lizzie not long after. How long after?"

"Didn't she tell you?" Walter gave a sly smile. "She wasn't attacked, neither. She wanted what we were going to give her, all three of us. Would have had us too if that one hadn't come along and spoiled her fun."

"Your fun, you mean," said Bel, still keeping her distance. "It didn't look like much fun for Lizzie."

"Maybe that's what she tells you now, but we know different." It was Walter doing all the talking now. Symon sat there slab-faced and sullen, angry about something, but he was angry about something most of the time.

"I suppose I'd better go and ask your father what time you came in, then," Thomas said to Symon, and saw the boy scowl.

"Pa was at The Star till late. I was asleep by the time he got home." He looked past Thomas. "I expect Bel can tell you what time he left."

Thomas glanced briefly at Bel, who shook her head. Symon's jibes meant nothing to either of them. Thomas wondered if last night had changed anything or not.

"So what time was it?"

"None of your business." Walter stood and made a show of brushing his backside down even though there was no mud on the milestone. "We don't have to tell you anything." He grinned and turned away, making for the town centre. Symon remained where he was for a moment, then rose to his full height, which brought him towering over Thomas.

Symon came forward so they were almost touching. Thomas saw his fist close, a tension in his shoulder, and when the punch came, he simply swayed and ducked beneath it. He made no attempt to respond, and Symon shook his head as if surprised Thomas was still on his feet.

"I don't want to hurt you," Thomas said.

Symon laughed. "That's good then, because I don't suppose you can. I want to hurt you, though."

Another swing came, this time with the left hand, and Thomas did the same as before, then again as Symon brought his right after it, perhaps in the mistaken belief Thomas was as stupid as himself and wouldn't expect the second blow.

Thomas jabbed his own right fist out and caught Symon just under the breastbone. It was a sensitive point and Symon gasped, trying to draw air into his lungs.

"I told you I didn't want to hurt you," Thomas said. "Do you want more, or are you going to tell me what time Raulf left you?"

Symon bent at the waist, still having trouble drawing breath, and Thomas gave him a moment. He glanced at Bel, who stood watching with a flush on her cheeks.

When he judged Symon recovered enough, Thomas said, "I'm still waiting."

"Gone eleven," said Symon through a gasp. "The town bell had struck not long before. We parted in the market square and made our own way home. The next thing I know it's all over Lemster that Raulf is dead and you killed him. Why did you kill him, Tom? I know we had that falling out, but it was no reason to kill him."

"I didn't kill him."

"That's what you say, but you're the only one they's looking at."

"I say it too," said Bel.

"He paid you a sixpence to say that, did he? That and the other thing, I expect. Turned me down you did, even though my money's as good as anyone else's."

123

"Would've taken me too long to find your pecker if what Lizzie said's true."

Thomas saw Symon bunch his fists again and stepped between him and Bel. It felt good to have someone to protect. Made him feel like a man. He pushed at Symon's chest with the flat of his hand. "Go on, follow your cur. He'll be wondering where you've got to."

It took a few moments for a decision to work its way through Symon's sluggish thoughts, then he must have seen sense. He scowled as if Thomas hadn't heard the last of the matter and lumbered away.

"You'll have to watch yourself now, Tom," said Bel, taking his hand. "But I liked it when you were so strong with him. I didn't think you could do that." She laughed. "How did you? He's near twice as big as you."

"It's nothing to do with how big you are," Thomas said.

Bel giggled and covered her mouth with her hand. "If you say so, Tom. Are we going to talk to Lizzie now?"

"I should have been harder on her the last time. I need to know if she saw Raulf skulking around when she was with Osmund."

"Would that be proof?" Bel fell into step beside him, swinging their joined hands for all the world to see, making some kind of statement to the town. Heads turned as they passed, but Thomas barely noticed.

"It would if she repeated it in front of Peter Markel, but I'm not sure she'll do that."

"Are you sure Osmund Gifforde killed Raulf?"

"It makes sense, doesn't it? A fight between rival suitors, one rejected, one protective." He smiled. "I'll protect you, Bel. I'll always protect you, whatever comes."

She tightened her fingers through his. "I know you will, Tom. Why do you think I'm with you where everyone can see us? Things are going to change in Lemster, you see if I'm right."

Thomas knew word would get back to his father and mother. He could imagine what his father would say. What his father would do. No doubt it would involve a strap on Thomas's bare back, but he had no idea how his mother would respond. Would she say anything at all or keep her own counsel? She would know of Joan Brickenden's profession. Everyone knew of Joan's profession. But would his mother disapprove or not? Some wives would, he knew, but he had always believed his mother had an open mind and heart. He hoped she would approve, because he was starting to develop real feelings for Bel. He determined he would ask her soon what her feelings were for him. Better to have them out in the open now before he got too involved. Before he got his heart broken.

Like Raulf had got his heart broken.

Thomas nodded to himself. Yes, it made sense. It made a great deal of sense. All he had to do was prove it.

He planned on going straight to Lizzie's house, but as they passed through the market square, Thomas saw her on the far side. She stood outside a shop selling fresh meat, and he pulled Bel into the cover of an alleyway. She laughed and went with him, slipping her arms around his waist.

"Lizzie's over there. Behave yourself."

"If someone comes along, they'll go back the way they came," said Bel. She lifted on tiptoe. "You can kiss me if you want, that would be even better."

"Behave yourself," Thomas said again as he looked over Bel's head to where Lizzie was passing a coin to the meat-seller.

"Why ever would I want to do that with you, Tom? What's she doing?"

"Buying meat. Mutton, I'd wager."

Bel giggled. "You'd know all about mutton I expect, what with all those sheep your father raises."

Bel's words reminded Thomas of the lost note of promise. Both the original and his forged note. It had represented a great deal of money and he felt bad about it, but there was nothing he could do about it now. He watched as Lizzie put the wrapped joint of meat into her woven bag and started toward the western side of the square. He extricated himself from Bel's clutches and took her hand again. Yes, let the whole town see them together. Get used to the idea, Lemster, for this girl is mine now. It brought a warm glow that Thomas tamped down. He could give full rein to his feelings for Bel when he had time. When he had proven his innocence.

They followed Lizzie as she took the path beside the Priory wall, overhung with birch and yew, the scent of it strong in the air. Thomas expected her to sense them and turn, but she continued on, oblivious to their presence.

"What are you going to do?" Bel asked, her voice low even though Lizzie was too far ahead to hear them if they spoke normally.

"After the bridge over the Kenwater, she'll either take the Hereford road or cross the fields. If she takes the fields, which I think she will because it's a quarter mile shorter to her house, we'll catch her up and confront her."

Bel squeezed his hand and Thomas increased his pace. His plan might have worked, but as they passed the end of the Priory wall, three figures stepped through a gate and Thomas stopped dead in his tracks. The tallest of the three looked up and a flash of anger crossed the familiar face.

"Where the fuck have you been?" John Berrington

walked fast to where Thomas stood with Bel's hand still clasped inside his.

Thomas released Bel and backed away. John Berrington glanced at the girl and scowled, then laughed. "Well, at least you haven't been wasting your time. Where did you get the money from, Tom?"

"No money, Squire Berrington," said Bel. "Me and Tom are in love."

John Berrington laughed all the harder. "Love, is it? Like your ma loves all the men in Lemster, I expect." He grabbed Thomas behind the neck and dragged him to where the other two men were watching proceedings with amusement. "You wanted to see Tom, didn't you, Peter?" He pushed Thomas forward. "Well here he is, late but no matter, and he's all yours. Do whatever you will with him, he's no son of mine anymore." He gave a final glance at Bel and strode away.

Peter Markel stared at Thomas. The man beside him, John Talbot, Earl of Shrewsbury, stood easily, waiting for his man.

"Do you need me for this, Peter?" he asked.

"It would be good if you could be present, sire. If we find the boy guilty you can call for a hanging today to save any waiting around."

John Talbot looked toward where Thomas's father had disappeared. "What about John?" he asked. "This is his son, is he not?"

"He is."

"Won't John want him pardoned? I can do that as easy as have him strung up. That might be the better solution. If he's guilty, of course."

"That is what we are about to decide, sire. The Prior has

gathered twelve men willing to act in judgement. Your wisdom will be much appreciated."

"As long as it's not going to take long. I have other business to conduct here before we return north, and the day is passing."

"I don't believe it will take long, sire. Most of us have already made up our minds on the matter."

When Thomas looked back, Bel had gone. Abandoned him to save herself, not that he blamed her, even though it hurt.

He followed the two men into the Priory grounds, knowing that to run would be an open admission of guilt. He was angry at his father's dismissal of him, but considered it no great loss. It might even be a boon if he lived to see nightfall, because then he would be free to be with Bel.

CHAPTER SIXTEEN

The room was different to the last time Thomas had been there. Now a group of twelve men of the parish sat on chairs to one side. The three arranged behind the long table remained as before. John Talbot stood in the corner with his arms crossed, an expression on his face letting everyone know this had better be quick or he wasn't going to hang around.

Peter Markel read from a sheet of paper, presumably notes made at the previous session. He glanced up at Thomas, at the men of the jury.

"I assume there are no more witnesses? I see that a Lizzie Martin was being sent for when we broke. Is that still relevant?"

Nobody spoke. Thomas didn't think it his place to say anything despite the threat to his life. He feared in that he was probably wrong.

"In that case," said Peter Markel, "we can ask the men of the jury if they have come to a conclusion in the accusation against Thomas Berrington." He glanced at them. "I understand you have been told of our deliberations. Have you reached a consensus?"

One of the men nodded. The others shifted, as if uneasy at whatever their verdict might be. All were men Thomas knew. Several worked for his father, several others Thomas considered might even like him; several he knew hated him. Among them was Symon Dawbney's father and Hugh Gifforde. Both would be happy to see him hang, guilty or not.

"Please tell me what your verdict is, then." Peter Markel's request was sharp, as if he had expected the verdict to be offered, not asked for.

As the man who had nodded rose, a commotion came from beyond the open doorway of the room. There were raised voices, one of them familiar to Thomas: that of Bel Brickenden.

"You have to let her tell what she knows!"

"What is going on out there?" demanded Peter Markel.

One of the monks shuffled in. "A girl claims there is a new witness. Another girl." The last said with dismissal, as if the word of a female was not to be taken seriously.

"The verdict is about to be given, tell them they are too late."

The monk gave a bow of his head and started to back out of the room.

"Wait." John Talbot pushed away from the wall and stood tall. "If there is new evidence it should be heard. We ought not hang a boy until we are sure of his guilt." He glanced at Peter Markel, who nodded. There was little else he could do. John Talbot owned him, down to the leather on the soles of his boots.

"Send them in then, if we must."

Bel came in, dragging Lizzie Martin behind her. Thomas

saw she was a reluctant witness, and feared what she might say. Bel's face was flushed, most likely from the effort.

"What do you have to tell us, girl?" said Peter Markel, mistakenly addressing his words to Bel, who pushed Lizzie forward.

"'Tis her, sir. She saw Raulf on Cursneh Hill the night he died."

"She did, did she?" Peter Markel nodded to the standing juror, indicating he could sit. "Tell me what you saw and make it quick."

John Talbot stepped back and leaned once more into the corner, his face expressionless.

Bel pushed at Lizzie, and Thomas wondered how she had persuaded her to come here. Promise or threat? He knew not which, only that she was here now. Lizzie glanced toward Thomas and his spirits rose as he saw a spark of forgiveness in her eyes. Bel must have told her something.

"I was on Cursneh Hill the night Raulf was killed," Lizzie said, her shoulders back and head up. She half turned between the men behind the table and the seated jurors. "Raulf came along bothering us and there was a fight."

Peter Markel made a brief note and leaned forward. "Bothering you? Who were you with, girl?"

Lizzie glanced at Bel, who gave a brief nod.

"Osmund Gifforde, sire."

"I'm no sire, girl. Sir will do." He glanced at the jurors, at Hugh Gifforde beside him, and Thomas knew he was calculating whether the man could remain where he was or not. Then he looked away. It would take too long to fetch someone else and brief them on all that had happened. "I won't ask what the pair of you were up to on this hill," he said to Lizzie. "Tell us what happened."

"Raulf came up after us, all riled. I used to walk out with

131

him, but I told him I didn't want to see him any longer. I told him I was walking out with Osmund now." She waited, as if expecting another question. When nothing came, she went on. "Raulf was fair angered, I tell you. Him and his so-called friends tried to … tried to hurt me earlier that night. I went and told Osmund and he took me up the hill to … to calm me down. Then Raulf comes shouting and cussing fit to burst. He pushed at Osmund even though he's older and bigger. Then Raulf pulled a knife on him and Osmund laughed."

Thomas saw Hugh Gifforde smile, perhaps proud of his son.

"Raulf tried to stick Osmund, but he wasn't fast enough. Nowhere near fast enough. Osmund took the knife from him and punched him on the face. Near broke his nose, I reckon."

"Did this Osmund use the knife on Raulf?" asked Peter Markel.

A look of shock showed on Lizzie's face. A face Thomas had once thought pretty until he fell in love with Bel.

"Of course not, sire. He handed the knife back to Raulf and pushed him away. Osmund told Raulf I was with him now and he'd better not come near me again or he'd be a dead man."

"He did, did he?" Peter Markel's lips thinned.

"He didn't mean it, sire. It was only said in anger, and to protect me. Osmund asked me to marry him. He said he'd asked his father and he was going to ask mine on the morrow. I said yes I would. Marry him, that is."

"All very lovely. But what happened to Raulf Wodall after he was given his knife back?"

"He slunk off, sire."

"Slunk off?"

"Osmund followed after him for a while to make sure he didn't try to sneak back on us. I was worried he might come back when I was alone up on the top of the hill. The sun was about to go down and I was afeared, but Osmund wasn't too long before he returned. He walked me all the way to my front door, he did, and then he went home."

Peter Markel stared at Lizzie. "How long was Osmund Gifforde away from you?"

"No more than a quarter hour, sire, I swear it."

"When he returned, was there any blood on him?"

Lizzie glanced away, her eyes downcast.

"Answer me, girl."

"He had blood on his shirt, sire, but he told me it was from when he hit Raulf."

Peter Markel sighed and washed a hand across his face. Once more he glanced at Hugh Gifforde, and this time he said, "Hugh, you need to excuse yourself." Next he looked toward John Talbot. "We should send for this Osmund boy, My Lord. He needs to be questioned at the least. There was a knife and more than enough time for him to take it from Raulf again and use it. And they were both of them on Cursneh Hill where the body was found."

John Talbot took a moment to consider the request, then nodded. "Do it, Peter. Have Thomas Berrington taken somewhere secure and send for the boy. I will have to leave you to your deliberations, but I will return for the verdict. How long will you be, Peter, one hour, two?"

"Best give us two, My Lord."

John Talbot nodded and strode from the room. A moment later, Brother Bernard entered. He twisted the rope around Thomas's wrists and led him away.

* * *

The cell had not changed in the days since Thomas last sat in it, other than the light fell on a different wall because it was still not yet noon. He wondered whether he would see the sun set this day. Brother Bernard had left him alone with his thoughts, which was perhaps a cruel thing to do.

As it turned out, not so cruel because before long, Thomas heard the approach of footsteps and the door opened. Brother Bernard appeared and walked to where Thomas sat and did his magic trick to make the rope spring loose.

"I brought a friend," he said, and left.

A moment later, Bel came in, a smile on her face. She ran to Thomas and embraced him so strongly they both ended up sprawled across the narrow cot. Thomas closed his hands around her narrow waist, the touch of her almost burning him. He lifted her away until she was sitting beside him. A far more acceptable place considering they were locked in a monk's cell.

"Thank you for fetching Lizzie, but I don't suppose it will do any good. Did you see their faces?"

"I did, but don't worry about it. That monk who brought me here told me he has been called to be on the bench"

"Brother Bernard?"

"Is that his name?" Bel smiled. "I like him. He's strong, like you. Not here," she squeezed his arm, her touch again burning, "but here as well." She touched his chest over his heart, then his forehead. "I expect he has a past, doesn't he?"

"He told me he fought the Moors in Spain," Thomas said. "He has travelled through a dozen lands. He has walked on solid ice in mountains and on burning sands in deserts. Yes, you should like him, for he is a good man. Is he really to be on the bench beside the other two?"

"He is."

Thomas felt a small sense of hope spark inside him.

"He knows the charges against you and there is no one else available who does. The Prior objected, but Peter Markel overrode him. He did ask the man if he was willing to serve and he said he was. He won't vote for your guilt, I know it."

"Did he say as much?"

Bel shook her head. "Of course not. He couldn't, could he? How long do we have, Tom?" She came closer, if such was possible.

Thomas knew that Brother Bernard would make his decision on the evidence. He liked Thomas well enough, but he was an honest man. Too honest to vote against his conscience because of friendship.

Bel took his hand again, her grip warm.

"Are you all right?" he asked. He lifted a hand and placed it against her cheek, which was also hot.

"I've a headache, and my bones ache." She grinned. "It's your fault for keeping me awake last night. How could I sleep with you lying right next to me?"

Thomas shook his head, recognising the lie, but pleased she at least tried.

"We can practise sleeping side by side some more if I ever get out of here."

Bel kissed him, but that was all. After a while, she lay on the cot and fell asleep. Thomas stood and walked to the high window and pulled himself up. He saw monks crossing the square. He leaned over as far as possible, but couldn't quite see the sundial he knew stood out there. From the position of the shadows, noon had come and gone. He lowered himself and sat in the corner of the cell. He watched Bel sleep, a smile on his face which faded when he

135

realised that come sunset, she might be the last thing he saw.

Brother Bernard came for them after an hour, but instead of tying his wrists with the cord, he told Thomas to sit on the bed beside the waking Bel and went to one knee in front of him.

"What is it?" Thomas asked.

"I have been talking to the other jurors to find out what they think, and it's not good, Tom. Every one of them thinks you killed Raulf."

Thomas stared at the man, his grizzled face and badly cut hair. "And what do you think?"

"I know you didn't kill him," said Brother Bernard. "But it doesn't matter what I think. Word has come down that ten men are enough to convict."

"For a hanging? I thought it had to be all twelve."

"As it should be, but things are happening out there and Peter Markel needs to leave today, as soon as he can. He wants a quick decision so he said ten men are enough. It will make no difference what I think. I believe Hugh Gifforde might have given them promises, or there were threats made before he left."

"Why? What has he got against me?"

Brother Bernard shook his head. "There are many folk in Lemster who don't like your family, Tom, you must know that. Your father and brother are both hard men, and I suspect you are tainted by association."

"So tonight I hang?" A sense of doom settled through Thomas, which Bel taking his hand again did nothing to lessen.

"More than likely. If you are still here, that is." Brother Bernard rose to his feet. "It has been good knowing you, Thomas Berrington."

"You too." Tears gathered behind Thomas's eyes and he fought to hold them back. He didn't want to show weakness in front of this man, whose strength had always been a beacon to him.

"God bless you. And if someone foolish should forget to lock the door behind them when they leave this room, it would only make sense for anyone meant to be imprisoned in it to take advantage of that foolishness and flee these parts as fast as they can."

Thomas stared up at Brother Bernard, but all he did was scowl. "You wouldn't be that foolish, would you, Tom?"

Thomas shook his head.

"I thought not. Have a good life, my son."

After Brother Bernard had gone, Thomas made himself wait long minutes before rising. When he tried the door, he discovered that some less than foolish man had indeed left it unlocked. He motioned Bel to join him and took her hand as they stepped into the corridor. From the far end came muffled conversation from the room where his trial was taking place, and he turned in the other direction. A narrow door at the end of the corridor opened without difficulty and Thomas found himself beyond the shaded northern wall of the Priory.

"Are we going to run away together, Tom?" Bel's hand clutched his even tighter than he grasped hers.

"Soon. I can't run without saying goodbye to my mother. I can't. You should go and do the same. You can pass through the town, nobody will be looking for you. Go now. I'll come for you when it gets dark and we'll flee into Wales. Nobody's going to come looking for us there."

"Can we get married, Tom?"

He laughed. "I hear over the border all you need to do is leap naked over a stream, so yes, I expect so."

"I like the sound of that. It might even cool me down some. I'm burning up, Tom." She kissed his mouth, then ran off. Thomas watched until she disappeared around the corner of the long wall that enclosed the Priory grounds, then made his way across the fields to home.

CHAPTER SEVENTEEN

When Thomas entered the house, Catherine Berrington looked up from where she was feeding wood onto the stove in the small ground floor room. Manor the house might be called by his father, but large it was not.

She smiled and rose, pushing her fists into the small of her back.

"Did they let you go, then, Thomas?"

He shook his head. "Me and Bel have got to run away. Well, I have to, and Bel says she wants to come with me."

"Bel Brickenden?"

Thomas nodded.

"Are you sure? You know she's—"

"I know what her mother is, but Bel's not her mother. We're in love."

He saw his mother suppress a smile and knew she didn't believe his words. "Are you now? Well, that's all right then, isn't it? Does your father know?"

"Sort of," Thomas said.

"Ah, it's like that, is it?"

"He knows, Ma. Brother Bernard told me they plan to hang me before sunset if I'm still in Lemster. I came to say goodbye. I couldn't leave without seeing you. I couldn't." Thomas felt the tears he had hidden from Brother Bernard squeeze past any attempt at restraint.

Catherine Berrington came across the room. Finally she believed him, Thomas saw, believed he had to run. There was no other choice. She embraced her son, pulling him against her. She was hot, like Bel. Thomas didn't think the day had been as warm as all that.

"Angnes is sleeping upstairs. Go and wake her to say goodbye. She'll be sore upset if you don't."

"Are you sure, Ma?" Thomas spoke against his mother's shoulder, knowing his tears were wetting the cotton of her dress.

"You need to, Thomas. You need to say your goodbyes, but when this all blows over, you are to come back here. Not to live, perhaps, but I want you to visit now and again. You'll be a man by then, married to Bel, I expect with children of your own, so don't you forget. Raising a family can make a man forget all the promises he made himself when he was young. Don't be like that, Thomas." She kissed the top of his head. "I love you. I will always love you." She patted his backside. "Now go and say goodbye to Angnes, and try not to make her cry too much."

When Thomas came back downstairs, he found his mother curled into a corner of the room, a hand clutched over her belly. She had vomited down her skirt and her face was as pale as winter snow. Thomas went to her, knelt and felt her face. She was burning up, hotter than even Bel had been, and the thought came to him that he knew what was wrong with her. There had been rumours of the pestilence

140

in Gloucester in the Spring. People said it came from London, or France, or Wales. Came from somewhere, in any case.

"Here, Ma, let me help you up to bed."

"Your father will be home soon and he'll want food. Just help me to the stove."

"You can't, Ma. Come on." Thomas put his arm beneath hers and tried to lift her and his mother cried out.

Thomas let her down to the floor again and felt beneath her armpit, afraid when he found three hard nodules there.

"You stay where you are, Ma, you'll be fine there."

Thomas rose and went upstairs to the bedroom his parents shared. He gathered up the mattress and a blanket and heaved them down the narrow stairs. He set up a makeshift bed in front of his mother, then rolled her onto it. With a slight feeling of guilt, he untied her dress and drew it down so he could check beneath her arms. The swelling he saw there only confirmed what he already knew.

"How long have you been like this, Ma?"

She was barely aware, drifting in and out of consciousness. Thomas went outside and filled a pail with cold well-water and carried it back in. He wetted a cloth and wiped her face and neck, wiped beneath her arms, but he knew no amount of water could cure what ailed her. His mother would live or die, only God knew which. Thomas certainly didn't.

When the rumours of pestilence reached the town, Thomas had asked Brother Bernard, because whenever there was something he didn't understand, he always asked Brother Bernard. The man, he knew, must have endless patience with him. Bernard had told him what to watch out for, but also said there was no known cure. At least five in ten who fell sick died. Thomas thought about that now. Five in ten sounded bad, but it also meant another five in ten might survive.

He wiped his mother's face again, made her sit up and drink something, and then John Berrington and his brother, the other John Berrington, came in.

"What the fuck are—" Thomas's father stopped dead in his tracks. "What's wrong with her?"

"You know what's wrong."

"It's in the town already? I thought out here we'd be safe."

"Except you and John have been in and out of town every single day. Did you think you were to be spared? Did you?" Thomas's anger welled up and he launched himself at his father, his fists flying.

The next thing he knew, he was coming around on the hard floor, lying beside his mother, and they were alone. Upstairs, little Angnes began to cry.

Thomas went upstairs and carried his sister down. He sat her in a chair well away from their mother before going back to her.

"I have to go out, Ma, but I'll be home as soon as I can. You lie there and get better." He pushed the pail of water close. "There's water here, and I'll cook food for us all when I get back."

His mother didn't stir. He had no idea if she had heard him or not.

Thomas picked Angnes up, set her on one hip and walked through the door.

When he reached the Brickenden house, everything was quiet. As Thomas walked through Lemster, people stayed back from him. Perhaps they had heard the news. Perhaps even from his father. Thomas wondered if he was in one of the myriad inns, drinking himself senseless, or doing his civic duty as the Earl's man in Lemster.

Thomas went up the stairs to Bel's room, praying she would laugh at him for bringing Angnes, but when he opened the rickety door, Bel was lying on her bed with sweat beading her body. When Thomas lifted her arm, he found the same swellings his mother had shown, scarce able to believe how fast the pestilence had struck the town. This morning she had woken beside him, and now she was fighting for her life. He sat Angnes in one corner, hemmed in with two chairs, and went downstairs and into the house.

Joan Brickenden sat in a chair, her breath coming in gasps. Her skin was waxy and pale. How could the world change so suddenly? Happy at sunrise, broken at sunset, and sunset still remained two hours away.

Adam Brickenden sat at the kitchen table. It was clear he was trying to be strong, but his face was as pale as his wife's, even though he appeared not to be sick.

"Have you come to take Bel away, boy?"

"I was going to," Thomas said. "But Ma's sick and Bel is. Your wife too."

"Bel's been sweet on you a long time now, Tom. Just try not to turn out like your father, or you'll have me to answer to. Do you promise me that, boy?"

"I promise it," Thomas said.

"Good enough. You have our blessing then, once Bel's well again. Me and Joan will dance at your wedding."

Thomas didn't know what to do, stay and nurse Bel or return home to nurse his mother. In his heart he knew there was only one answer, but it wasn't the one he wanted to acknowledge. He returned to Bel's room to discover Angnes waddling across the floor on her sturdy legs. His little sister was barely two years old, sweet-natured like her mother, adventurous like her brother. Like one of them, anyway. Thomas scooped her up before she could reach Bel and plonked her down in the corner again, knowing even if she started across once more, he had time enough for what he had to do.

He knelt beside Bel and lifted her hand to his lips. She roused a little and tried to smile.

"Don't you go sweet-treating me now, Tom. You know I need to sleep until I'm better."

Five in ten, Thomas thought. Which would Bel be?

"I have to go out," he said. "Ma's sick. Sicker even than you. I've brought you water and some cloths, and I'll come back as soon as I can, but I have to go."

"I understand," said Bel, her voice little more than a whisper. "Take all the time you need, and send her my love."

"I will."

Thomas leaned over and kissed Bel on the lips. Even as he did so, he knew it was stupid, but he had to say goodbye properly. When he rose, Angnes was on her way across the floor again and he lifted her up and ran down the stairs. Striding along the road, he put a hand to his sister's brow, relieved to find it cool. Angnes laughed and tried to raise her own hand, but couldn't reach his. Thomas lifted her so she could, then kissed her belly to make her laugh.

His mother was worse, worse still when finally his father and brother staggered in. So no civic duty, then. They glanced at the makeshift bed but said nothing before climbing the stairs. Thomas left them to it, not caring a jot about either of them. He washed his mother again in the candlelight, then brought a chair close and sat, watching the face he knew better than his own. He watched the way her eyes moved beneath their closed lids and wondered what she was dreaming about. Something happy, he hoped.

When he opened his eyes again, the first grey light of dawn was leaching into the room and his mother lay at peace, but it was the peace of the dead. Thomas felt her neck as Brother Bernard had taught him, then laid a hand on her chest, but there was nothing. How could she go so fast? he thought. Alive one day, gone the next, giving him no time to prepare. Grief ran through him, making his knees weak when he needed to be strong.

He went to where Angnes lay in her cot, which he had brought downstairs, relieved to find she was still cool to the touch. Thomas felt his own brow and found it the same as that of his sister. He went out to the barn to find a spade and began to dig. All the Berringtons for four generations back lay in the small graveyard on the slope above the house. A final resting place where they could look across the town and beyond to distant Welsh hills. It was from there his father claimed they had come from. Just like John Tudor's family. Just like King Henry's ancestors had.

Thomas's brother John came down with a fever the following day. He died two days later.

His father fell ill, but recovered, only to complain that Thomas had done a poor job of the crosses on the newly dug graves, but Thomas had stopped caring what his father thought.

Only when he was sure John Berrington wouldn't die and there was no need for another grave to be dug, only when he was sure Angnes continued to be healthy, did he walk through an almost deserted Lemster, where doors were shut and barred to keep out the sickness, and make his way to see Bel. By then, of course, he was too late. She was already lying in a new bed, with freshly dug earth as her blanket.

Adam Brickenden came from the house.

"How is your wife?" Thomas asked.

"She's turned a corner, I think. She'll live."

"I loved her," Thomas said.

"My wife? I ought to thrash you, boy."

"Bel."

"I know who you meant." Adam Brickenden wouldn't meet his eyes and Thomas knew something was wrong.

"She's gone," said Adam Brickenden, and Thomas glanced at the field beyond the works where this family had their graveyard. Adam Brickenden saw his look and shook his head. "No, she's not there, though God knows why not. She was bad, real bad. She's gone into Wales to her aunt."

"Wales?"

Adam Brickenden lifted a hand and pointed west. "It's that way."

"I know where Wales is. Why did she go? She knew I was coming back for her, didn't she?"

"You should go and talk to Joannie about why Bel went, but if you think on it, I'm sure you can work it out for yourself. Bel tells me you're a clever lad. Too clever for her."

Thomas knew he had no need to talk to Joan Brickenden. He knew why Bel had gone into Wales. She was running away—from him.

"Where does her aunt live in Wales?"

"Bel told me you'd ask that. She also told me not to tell you."

"I can go and find out, you know."

"You can try, but if Bel doesn't want you finding her, you won't. She did leave me a message for you. If you came, she said."

"Of course I was going to come. Did she think I would abandon her?"

"Aye, she said she thought you would come."

"What was the message?" Thomas didn't know if it would be the kind of thing Adam Brickenden would want to pass over to him.

"She said, 'Tell Tom to be the best he can.'" Adam Brickenden offered a smile. "And then she said, 'And tell him to take no shit from nobody.'"

"That sounds like Bel," said Thomas.

"Aye, it does." Adam Brickenden clapped Thomas on the shoulder. "You know it's for the best this way, Tom, don't you?"

"What do you think?"

"Don't matter what I think, Tom. How are your folks, anyway?"

"Ma's gone. So is John. Father caught it, but got better."

"And the little one? I forget her name."

"Angnes. She never got sick, just like I never got sick."

Adam Brickenden started to turn away, stopped. "What happened with all that trouble you were in? Did it get sorted out?"

"I suppose it did, one way or another."

Thomas went to the Priory, curious himself if his trouble was sorted out or not. Brother Bernard came out to see him, closing the entrance door behind him.

"Are they sick inside?" Thomas asked.

"Some. Not all."

"You?"

Brother Bernard shook his head. "I caught the sickness in the Holy Land and recovered. I believe once you've had it, you don't get it a second time, but what do I know?"

Thomas smiled. "More than anyone else around here."

"Yes, well, you don't know everybody, do you, Tom? What about you?"

"Nothing. Bel caught it, but got better and now she's run off to Wales so she can avoid me. She thinks she'll ruin my life, but she's wrong."

"I heard she'd gone. I hear most things."

"Did you hear anything about the accusation against me? What's happening with that?"

"John Talbot and Peter Markel couldn't get out of Lemster fast enough when they heard the sickness was here, though I expect it will follow them to Shrewsbury soon enough. Might even have come from there. Might have been them who brought it here." Brother Bernard stretched and looked up at the sky, which was a pale blue with white clouds off to the west. A pleasant day, if it wasn't for everything that had happened. "What are you going to do now, Tom?"

"I don't know. Maybe I'll become a monk and join you."

Brother Bernard laughed and cuffed him around the head. "Do you believe in God Almighty?"

"I thought I did. After what's happened, I'm not so sure anymore."

"Ah well, it's not essential if a boy wants to join us, but it helps. As for me, I know there is something, but the idea of a God sitting up there?" He nodded at the sky. "That I'm not so sure of." He tapped his own chest. "If there is a God, I believe He sits in here, inside us, men and women both. Maybe even in animals, I don't know. He makes us do good."

"So how does that explain those who don't? How does that explain whoever killed Raulf?"

"There is always the Devil, Tom. Beware of him."

"I'll try."

Thomas was walking home across the field toward where he had seen the three boys blocking his passage across the Lugge when a rangy figure came running over the grass toward him. He recognised Osmund Gifforde and began to run himself. He feared with the chaos in the town, Osmund might take the opportunity for some manner of revenge.

"Hold up, Tom, I need a word."

Thomas half-turned to see how far Osmund was behind him, caught his foot on a tussock and went flying through the air. When he rolled over, Osmund loomed above him, but he extended a hand in an offer to help him up. Thomas took it and got to his feet.

"How are your folks?" he asked.

"We're most of us hale. We locked ourselves away as soon as we heard, and only Walter's come down with it. He's why I'm here. He wants to see you."

"Me? What for?"

"Don't know. All I know is he said, 'Fetch Tom', so here I am."

Thomas fell in with Osmund as they made their way back across the fields toward town.

"Have you been looking after him?"

"Somebody has to. The others sent him out to the barn as soon as he got the fever. They'd have left him there on his own. They're all too afraid to help."

"So you helped him?"

"Like I said, someone has to."

"Lizzie?" Thomas asked.

"Haven't seen her. Haven't heard anything either. I plan on going over there once I've taken you to see Walter."

"He's in the barn, you said?"

Osmund Gifforde nodded.

"Then go and see her, I know my way to your barn. I don't expect your brothers will try to beat me again, will they?"

"Scared is what they are. Cowards, all of them." Osmund thumped Thomas on his back. "You're a good man, Tom Berrington. I hope you and Bel will be happy together." Clearly he hadn't heard the news of her flight.

CHAPTER EIGHTEEN

Thomas saw nobody as he walked through Lemster toward the Gifforde farm. Doors remained closed throughout the town. Behind them, men, women and children huddled or suffered, and if they suffered, they kept their suffering to themselves. An hour of daylight remained, but the golden beauty of the evening did nothing to soften the terror that gripped everyone. Thomas went directly to the barn, not caring if those inside the house saw him or not. Inside he looked around, the air dim, redolent with hay and the scent of dried dung from the animals kept there.

"Walter?" Thomas called out, unable to see the boy he had once called a friend. He had an idea of what Walter wanted to see him about. A few days earlier it might have made him angry. Now only sadness filled him.

"Stay away from me, Tom." Walter's voice came from a dark corner, and as Thomas moved in that direction, it sounded more firmly. "I said stay away! I've got the sickness."

Thomas kept moving. "I've spent days looking after my mother and brother and I'm not sick. I don't expect getting near you is going to make much difference." Even as he spoke the words, he wondered whether he believed them or not. The sickness had come fast to the town, but he knew it must have been festering inside those who caught it for days. Perhaps the travellers had brought it when they came for the May Fair. It could have been anyone passing through, or someone who had visited Ludlow or Hereford. The sickness crept silently through the land with no rhyme or reason to it. People had theories, but Thomas believed none of them. Sickness just was. There was no cure and no hiding. You caught it or you didn't. You lived or you died.

Walter Gifforde leaned into the corner of the barn, his body supported on soft straw, a stained blanket covering him to the neck.

"Do you have the swelling?" Thomas asked, and Walter nodded. "Osmund said you wanted to see me. Why?"

"You know why, Tom. I'm dying and I need to make my peace with God and you before I go. I could do with a priest, but they're not going to come out here, are they?"

"I could go and ask Brother Bernard. He might."

"He's not a priest, though, is he?"

"No, he's not, but he does know about healing. He's shown me some things I used with Ma and John." Thomas looked around. "Not that they did much good." He looked back at Walter. "Besides, you might not die. Not everybody does. Might be best to keep whatever you want to tell me to yourself until you know one way or the other."

Walter made a sound almost like a laugh, if not for the rattling in his chest when he made it. "Well, we both know if I end up one of those ways, it's going to be too late, so best I do what's right now." Walter looked up and met Thomas's eyes. "I should have spoken sooner when you were arrested, but Father told me not to. Threatened me with a beating if I did." Walter waited a moment, each breath appearing to be an agony. "Have you ministered to others, Tom?"

Thomas nodded.

"Did you cure any of them?"

"My father, I suppose. My mother and brother not."

"Will you help me?"

Thomas stared at the boy. He thought about him on the makeshift bridge over the Lugge, where all his problems had started. He could scarce believe he was looking at the same person. He believed he knew what Walter was going to tell him and a flare of anger surged through him. Walter Gifforde had always been a coward and Thomas didn't expect getting sick would have changed his ways. Still, he couldn't leave him to suffer, not now he knew about it. Thomas looked around, saw a wooden bucket banded with iron hoops near the door and went to it. Out in the yard, he used the pump to draw water into the bucket and carried it inside.

"You need to get out of those clothes so I can wash you. Staying clean seems to be one of the things that helps. At least that's what Brother Bernard told me, and he's the closest we have to a physician in Lemster."

"Heathen knowledge, Father says. Picked up beyond Mercia."

"I don't expect Mercia has any sovereign right to knowledge." Thomas set the bucket down. "Here, sit up, I'll help you."

For a moment he thought Walter was going to argue, but then he started to struggle upright and Thomas leaned over and helped him sit. When his clothes were piled on the floor, Thomas examined him, finding the swellings beneath his arms and in his groin as expected. The boy's skin also burned beneath his touch. Thomas lay him down and wiped at the grime on Walter's body with a cloth, the water cooling him if nothing more.

"Tell me what you brought me here for," he said, hoping his ministrations might soothe at least some of Walter's fear.

"I'm not so sure I should tell you, Tom. What if I get better? What if you go telling the Prior or that Peter Markel what I did? I'll be free of the pestilence only to hang."

"So it was you who killed Raulf."

Walter looked away. Thomas continued to wipe the cloth across his skin, cleaning away what looked like half a year's worth of grime. The pile of discarded clothing seemed to move of its own volition as lice jumped in search of fresh body-heat, and Thomas itched even as he was sure none had yet fed on him. He used a length of wood to pick up the clothes and toss them into a corner.

"I didn't mean to." Anguish showed on Walter's face, and Thomas almost believed him. "Will I hang, Tom?"

"Tell me exactly what happened, though it's not me who will judge you."

Walter tried to smile before abandoning the attempt. "Then I'm lucky, for you'd be happy to see me hang, wouldn't you?"

"Depends what you did, but I'd rather see nobody hang."

"I haven't told you what I did yet."

"I know the three of you attacked Lizzie Martin. Why did you do that? Did you think you could get away with raping her?"

"It was a jest, that's all. At the start, anyway. Then Symon got himself carried away and pulled his thing out." Another smile threatened to show before sinking back into the greyness of Walter's face. "Weren't so much of a threat, mind."

"I heard about that," Thomas said.

"He would've put it in her too if Bel hadn't come along. She's brave, that girl."

"She is that." They were all of them on the cusp of becoming men, and Bel had almost dragged him across that divide. There was no going back from the knowledge and delight of what they had almost had. Of what could have been. Thomas pushed his grief away, knowing he could give full rein to it later when he was alone. He needed to keep himself busy, needed to distract his thoughts.

"It started before then, though," said Walter. "We messed with Lizzie because we were all of us angered up, and that was your fault."

"My fault? How was it my fault? You're not about to change your story, are you?"

"No, I'll tell you the truth now. Whether I tell the same truth a week from now, who knows? There's nobody here but me and you, and I can say you made up everything I'm going to tell you. Who will they believe then? Me or the boy already accused?"

Thomas got to his feet and tossed the wet rag onto Walter's chest. "Then you can look after yourself. I've got things to be doing and places to be." He started to turn away.

"Don't, Tom. I'll tell you what we did, tell you what happened, but I don't want you judging me. It wasn't like I meant to kill Raulf. If you hadn't pushed me in the river, none of this would have happened."

"There you go—blaming me again." Thomas started to turn once more, but it was for show this time. He wanted to hear the rest of Walter's story. He was sure some would be a fabrication to show him in a better light, but he also knew it was going to be the closest he would ever come to an answer to what happened.

"They laughed at me," said Walter, his eyes not meeting Thomas's gaze. "They left me there in the river and laughed at me. Symon called me a girl. I wanted to hurt him so I came home and stole Ma's filleting knife. The sharp one."

"You wouldn't have used it," Thomas said.

"Do you think not? I was fair mad by then. Your fault again. But when I found Symon and Raulf, they just laughed at me again and I pulled the knife. All I saw was red in front of me and I planned to stick it in Symon first, but he knocked it away like it meant nothing, and then he hit me. And then..." Walter shook his head. Thomas waited for him to go on. "Then he put his arm around me and said he knew what would make a man of me."

"Lizzie," Thomas said.

Walter shook his head. "Not Lizzie. Bel Brickenden. He said she was the daughter of the town whore, so she must be a whore herself. He put a penny in my hand and said it would be more than enough."

"You went looking for Bel, not Lizzie?"

Walter nodded. "It was all Symon's idea, like nothing had ever happened, like we were all best friends again. But then as we were going into town, my father and brothers found us. Symon told them what you'd done to me and that was the reason they came looking for you, Tom."

"You didn't try to stop them, though, did you?"

"Why would I? If I couldn't stick Symon, then watching you take a beating was even better."

"What happened afterward? I assume you didn't find Bel?"

"We looked, but then Raulf saw Lizzie on her way home and said she'd be even better than Bel."

"Why?"

Walter shrugged. "He never said and I never asked. We

were all excited from watching you take that beating and we followed her. Symon ran ahead and dragged her into some bushes, but half of them were briars. Not that we noticed, not then. Our blood was up, and if Bel hadn't come along I think we'd all have taken a turn with Lizzie. I know Raulf would because he said she owed him, though he didn't tell me then she had spurned him for my brother."

"I thought it was Osmund had killed Raulf."

"I wish he had. Do you think this sickness is God's judgement on me, Tom, for killing Raulf? I never meant to do it."

"You took a knife to a fight, what did you think was going to happen?"

"I lost the knife when Symon knocked it out of my hand. I got a thrashing from Ma when she found it gone. She knew it must have been me who took it."

"You said Symon had taken you all to look for Bel?"

"He did."

"So you could rape her?"

Walter looked away.

"What happened when she came across you all? Bel's shorter than Lizzie and slighter of frame. What changed Symon's mind?"

"Have you seen Bel in a temper? God's teeth, Tom, she'd scare my pa into doing whatever she told him, and Pa's a hard man. I think Bel could take on anybody in this town with one hand tied behind her back. So we ran, all three of us. Except Raulf was the first to stop. He left us, told us he had something he had to do."

"Did he tell you what?"

"No."

"But you were close to Cursneh Hill, I bargain."

"Near the bottom of it, by that track that winds up through the trees. We left Raulf there."

"When did you confront him?"

"I didn't. It was the other way around. Symon had gone home by then and I was thinking about it, but I was still all riled up at what we'd done and thinking about girls and not much else. I was also wondering what Raulf was up to climbing Cursneh Hill, so I decided to follow him. I knew he used to walk out with Lizzie and I wondered if they'd made things up. I thought … I thought I might catch them doing things and see something."

"After what had happened?"

"I wasn't thinking straight. And when I got close, I saw Raulf fighting with Osmund. But it was a short fight before Osmund knocked him to the ground. Osmund followed him and I followed them both. If Raulf was going to get stuck, I wanted to see it. But they only had another fight. Osmund left Raulf on the ground and went back for Lizzie. They went down the hill. I hid when they passed, then went back to see if Raulf was all right, but he came spitting and cursing at me. Maybe he thought I was Osmund come back to finish him. Before I knew what was happening, he had a knife in his hand and he came at me with it. I thought I was dead, truly I did. Raulf is wily and fast and I knew I was no match for him."

"So what did you do?"

"I turned and ran as fast as I could. But he was faster. He caught me by the shoulder and held me back. I tripped and went flat on my face. Before I knew what was happening, Raulf was sitting on me and I think I probably screamed. I lashed out. I didn't go for the knife, Tom. I didn't even know what I was doing. But the next thing I know, Raulf's full weight is across me and I can barely move. I heaved and squirmed and he kind of fell sideways. When I got to my knees, the knife he was going to stick me with was buried in his chest. I didn't want to touch him, but I needed to know if he still lived. When I put my hand on his chest, it was still. I pulled the knife out and ran. Which is when I saw you making your way home. I knew I could get away with killing Raulf if someone else took the blame."

"Raulf was stuck more than once," Thomas said.

Walter wouldn't meet his eyes. "I needed to make it look like it was done in anger, didn't I?"

"It was you who hit me?"

"It wasn't nothing personal, Tom, anyone would have done the same. You just happened to be there and it made sense after the fight we had, after what you did to me and Raulf. I knew you'd get the blame if the knife was found on you."

Thomas shook his head. "There was no knife."

"I should never have tossed you in the river. It must have fallen out of your belt and the water took it. You should have drowned, Tom, then none of this would have happened. You were meant to drown."

Thomas sat back, staring at the fevered boy. "I thought we were friends."

"That was before I killed someone. What would you have done?"

"Owned up. It was Raulf who attacked you. You should have told the story and taken a whipping. They wouldn't have strung you up for self-defence."

"Raulf was a Wodall, Tom. You know how it works around here—you more than anyone, with you getting away with murder."

"Except I didn't commit any murder, remember. You did."

This time Walter managed to raise a smile. "Except nobody knows that except me and you, and if you tell anyone, I'll deny it all. There's no proof but your word, and nobody will take that anymore. Not now."

Thomas looked around. There were two pitchforks leaning against the wall of the barn, together with a heavy axe, its blade embedded in a cut log.

"I should kill you here and now," he said.

"You wouldn't. I know you, Tom, you don't kill people, you save them. We laugh about it between us. Saint Thomas Berrington. You and that monk. Does he touch you, Tom? I expect he does, doesn't he? It's not natural, all those men locked up together. It's what they do, everyone knows that. Does he put his—"

Thomas didn't let Walter complete his ravings. He punched him hard in the mouth, not sorry about it, only sorry it hurt his fist. Then he rose and left Walter to whatever fate the sickness had in store for him. Outside he looked at the windows of the farmhouse where candle-light now showed. He hesitated, almost going across to knock on the door, then turned away.

Two weeks, he thought. Two weeks was all it took for the world to fall apart.

CHAPTER NINETEEN

Thomas was in the field behind the house, putting fresh crosses on the graves of both his mother and brother when his father bellowed something indecipherable from inside. Thomas ignored him until he had completed his work, hammering the new crosses into the soft earth. They looked better than his first attempt. He bent his head and said a short prayer, though the words meant less than they had two weeks before. The God he once believed would protect him had abandoned them all.

Another bellow pulled him out of his misery and he trudged indoors, each footstep like lifting lead. His father sat in a chair near the fire, a blanket wrapped across his legs.

"What do you want, Pa?" Thomas stood in the doorway, waiting.

"She's crying again."

"She misses Ma."

"Well she'll have to get used to it, like the rest of us. Go and stop her, Tom, before she screams the brains from my head. Then get me some ale."

"You finished the ale last night."

"Then go into town and fetch me more. I've been sick, and nothing heals a man better than fresh ale."

"There won't be any in town either," Thomas said. "Over half the town got sick and half those who got sick died, Pa."

"There'll be ale for John Berrington. Take coin from upstairs and bring me some. But not until you've quieted Angnes, damn her. And bring me a cut of that meat before you go to her."

Thomas ignored the request and climbed the stairs. Angnes lay in her cot. She was wet and had soiled herself, so Thomas stripped his sobbing sister and washed her clean before finding fresh clothes. As he picked through the small pile of things, he picked out the best and stuffed them into a sack. He glanced at the bed his mother and father had once slept side by side in and felt something work loose inside his chest. He pushed it away, knowing he had to be strong. At least Angnes had stopped crying and he lifted her onto his hip and carried her downstairs. He took money from the small pile on the table, glanced at his father, who had gone to sleep, and walked outside.

He considered what to do next. He wasn't going to walk into Lemster to buy ale for his father. Instead he went to the barn and took down a saddle and bridle. He set the saddle on the ground, and Angnes on the saddle, which she thought was a fine game. He went into the field to call Bayard. The animal glanced up from where it was pulling at fresh grass, then plodded across. Thomas rubbed the charger's nose and slipped the bridle over its head. Bayard was enormous, but gentle, and a much better choice than either of the other two steeds. Once he was saddled, Thomas sat Angnes in front of the pommel, then pulled himself up. He reseated Angnes in front of him and kicked with his heels, guiding the horse out onto the Ludlow road.

"Where go, Toma?" Agnes asked. She had started talking a bare few months ago, as the leaves began to bud on winter-naked trees. Now Thomas could understand almost everything she said, even if she still had trouble with his name. Like his mother, Angnes never shortened it, only by accident rather than design.

"Aunt Jane's house."

Angnes laughed. She liked her aunt Jane, though it had been the turn of the year since the family had seen each other. Thomas wondered how hard the sickness had hit Ludlow and whether Jane Baxter, her husband and two children still lived. He hoped they did because he didn't know what he would do if not.

The road north was sweet with the scent of May blossom, soft with a westerly breeze. Orleton came and went without any sign of people, as did Richard's Castle and Overton. Eventually the bulk of Ludlow Castle showed ahead and Thomas reseated Angnes more securely in front of him, though she rarely stopped squirming, wanting to see everything and make comment on it.

"What hill?" "Who that?" "Where that?" Question after question, each of which Thomas tried to answer with patience.

On the outskirts of Ludlow, he stabled the horse at an inn and carried Angnes up the hill to the town centre, then set her down because she wanted to walk.

Jane and Roger's baker's shop was set on the main street and there were people buying their bread and sweet pastries. Aunt Jane looked up as Thomas approached. When she offered a wide smile, Thomas felt something loosen inside himself he hadn't even been aware of until that moment. He kissed his aunt on the cheek, enveloped by her familiar scent of flour and baking. She lifted Angnes and kissed her face until the girl laughed and squirmed to be put down, where she reached up once more for Thomas's hand.

"Only you, Tom?"

He nodded, and his aunt must have seen something on his face, heard something in his lack of words.

"Kate?" she asked, and Thomas nodded once more. All at once the tears filled his eyes. "Oh, Tom, my poor boy. Come inside." She grasped his free hand and drew him past the shop front and beyond to where the ovens sat. A steep stair led up to the Baxters' living quarters, but she didn't take them there. Instead they passed through the hot workroom to a small courtyard where apple and cherry trees grew, their fruit starting to form. A small wooden table and four chairs were set on flagstones.

"Tell me what happened," she said as she sat across from him. "We had the sickness here, but not so bad. A few died, but not many. Not like the last time. Was it worse in Lemster?"

"It was bad," Thomas said. "John's gone." When Aunt Jane showed shock, he raised a hand. "My brother John. Father got sick, but recovered. Ma went first. A lot in the town went the same way." Thomas thought of Bel, but knew he couldn't say anything about her to his aunt. There was no point. Nobody else needed to know, but Thomas's heart would carry her memory forever.

"What are you going to do?" His aunt glanced at Angnes, back to him, and Thomas watched her face for some sign she would reject his sister.

"I can't look after her, Aunt Jane, and you know Father won't. I don't know where else to take her."

She looked at Angnes, who had climbed down and was on hands and knees under the trees, looking for anything that might move.

"She'll be another mouth to feed."

"I can send money. I'll make sure Father does that, at least."

"There's talk of more war. The Earl is gathering men, they say. Has he come to Lemster yet?"

"Two weeks ago, not since." There was no point mentioning the accusation against himself.

"I expect he's going to want John with him, isn't he?"

"I don't know."

"What about you, Tom?" She glanced at Angnes again. "There's a place for you here if you want it. You'll have to work, but there'll be a roof over your head and food on the table every night."

"I can't leave Pa on his own."

"Will he even notice if you're not there? Does he miss Kate?"

"You know what he's like," Thomas said. "He's carved from oak, with a heart of iron. If John Talbot comes for him, he'll go, and willingly. More than willingly. Maybe when he does, I'll come back to Ludlow, but until then, he needs me. He's not used to managing for himself."

His aunt reached across and patted Thomas's hand. "You're a good boy. Kate will be proud of you. I'm sure she's watching over you from above." She crossed herself, then used the same hand to wipe a tear from the corner of her eye. "Come back if you need to. You are staying tonight, aren't you?"

Thomas shook his head. He glanced to where Angnes was using the garden wall to help herself stand while she peered into a hole in the lime mortar. He stood, leaned over and kissed his aunt, then turned away. Better not to make any fuss of his little sister. He was starting to learn that goodbyes were hard. Better Angnes enjoy the afternoon while she could.

* * *

"Did she take her?" John Berrington was on his feet, standing outside the house when Thomas rode up. He leaned on a stick, trying to make it appear as if it wasn't necessary.

"She did." Thomas slid off the saddle, a long way down to the ground, and patted the horse's flank.

"Make sure you rub him down with hay, and give him some extra feed."

"I will. Aunt Jane said John Talbot is gathering an army."

"He told me when he was here. He's going to call for me when he travels south."

"You told him you'd go?" Thomas heaved the saddle from the back of the horse and carried its weight into the barn. He came back with straw to wipe the sweat from the beast.

"Of course I told him I'd go. It's war, Tom. Those French think they can steal our legitimate land and we need to teach them another lesson. Damn, but this war has dragged on long enough. We go and beat them hard this time. Teach them the English are not to be messed with."

"What about me?"

"What about you?"

"I assume if John still lived he'd be coming with you."

John Berrington laughed. "Do you think I want to take you instead?" He shook his head. "You're no warrior, Tom. Too much reading." He tapped his brow. "Too much thinking. You can stay here with that girl of yours."

"Bel died."

"Ah well. Girls do. Boys as well. What would I want with

you? You'd have to look out for yourself. I wouldn't have time to watch over you."

Thomas looked around as he continued to wipe down the horse. "I can't stay here on my own, Pa."

"You could join the Priory. That Bernard would have you, I don't doubt."

"You have to believe in God for that," Thomas said.

John Berrington stared at his son. "Are you saying you don't, boy?"

"What kind of God would take Ma and John both, as well as Bel and half the town? What kind of merciful God is that?"

"Don't let anyone else hear you talk that way or you'll be in even more trouble than you already are."

"I'm not in trouble anymore. I know who killed Raulf."

"Do you, by God? Do you have proof?"

"That depends whether Walter lives or dies. He told me what happened. It was an accident, he says. Does that mean he'll hang or not?"

"Probably hang, accident or no. One boy's dead and another did it. I might have managed to get you off, Tom, but I doubt Hugh Gifforde can do the same for Walter. He'll hang, as sure as night follows day. If you tell anyone, that is." John Berrington stared at Thomas hard and long. He seemed to be waiting for something.

"You would have tried to get me off, Pa?"

John Berrington nodded. "I might not like you much, Tom, but you're still my son. I couldn't see you dangle." He let his breath go and shifted on his feet, repositioning the staff until he was more comfortable. "Promise me you'll stay out of the way and you can come. Don't get underfoot. Don't, whatever you do, say a single word to John Talbot. He doesn't take much to gabby boys. And try not to get yourself killed if you can. There's a mail vest of John's in the house, his sword and a couple of knives. I expect they're yours now if you want them."

Thomas wasn't sure he did, but nodded anyway. Anything not to be left alone.

"Can you cook?" his father asked.

"I don't know. I cooked that joint last night and you're still here. I've watched Ma and it doesn't look too hard. Why?"

"I'm hungry."

* * *

A mist hung across the fields as Thomas made his way through them toward the Gifforde farm. He skirted the house itself and made for the barn, unsure if he would find a corpse or a living body when he entered.

Walter was sitting up, pale but clearly recovering. Thomas went to him and lifted an arm, but Walter shook him off.

"They're going down."

"Then I suppose you'll live. Not that you deserve to."

Walter stared at him. "Those things I told you," he said. "You know I made them all up, don't you?"

"Did you?"

"Of course I did. I never killed Raulf. Symon did it. I saw it with my own eyes."

Thomas shook his head. "Have you heard something, then?"

"Heard something?"

"About Symon?"

"Someone did say he might have died. They drew straws in the house and Adam lost. He had to bring food out to me. He told me about Symon when he came. All the Dawbneys are dead, he said. Half the town is dead."

168

"It hit Lemster hard," Thomas said. "Did you tell Adam what you told me, or did you lie to him as well?"

"I told him the truth—that Symon killed Raulf."

"Did he believe you?"

"Of course he did. I'm his brother, aren't I? You're lucky I didn't tell him I saw you do it. I could have, just as easy as saying it was Symon, but you did come and help me when nobody else would."

"I'm leaving Lemster," Thomas said, turning away. He wanted nothing to do with the Giffordes. Nothing to do with the town anymore. There was nothing here for him.

* * *

There was only one person he couldn't leave without saying goodbye to.

It was a week later and John Talbot's rag-tag army was camped on the edge of town, gathering what few men from the district they could before marching south. There was talk of a ship from Gloucester, or maybe Bristol. Others said they would have to march as far as Plymouth to take ship, but everyone knew the end of their journey was Bordeaux, and war.

Brother Bernard was tending his herb garden when Thomas found him. He straightened and brushed down his robe.

"I wondered if I would ever see you again."

Thomas looked around at the neatly tended rows of plants. Brother Bernard had taught him what most were for, and Thomas thought he remembered at least some of it. "So you still didn't get sick?"

"I told you I came down with it once a long time ago, when I was in Aragon."

Thomas had no idea where that was. Not that it mattered.

169

"And the brothers?"

"Most are well enough. We keep to ourselves and wash often and it seems to have passed us by." He crossed himself. "Praise be to God."

"Yes," Thomas said. "Praise be to God. I'm leaving with Father when the army goes south."

"Where to?"

"France. Well, not France, Bordeaux. English land."

"What's left of it. You're no soldier, Tom."

"I know. But I can fight, and I'm fast, and you taught me a trick or two. I expect I'll manage." Or die more likely, but he kept that thought to himself.

Brother Bernard came across and put a hand on Thomas's head. "Aye, I reckon you will. Look after yourself, Thomas Berrington. I'm going to miss you. But not as much as you'll miss me."

"No," Thomas said, "not as much."

He waited for something, some embrace between friends, but Brother Bernard made no move and Thomas knew he couldn't. There was nothing to keep him, but still he stood facing the tall man who had once fought for his country and the Church. He thought of the tales told and the lessons learned and wiped tears from his eyes.

"Take care, Tom. Don't go getting yourself killed too easy."

"I'll try not to."

Thomas turned and walked across fields rich with grass until he came to the army camped alongside the Lugge. He went to find his father. He didn't look back. There was nothing left for him in Lemster. His future, if he had one, lay elsewhere. He was going to war and expected he'd be one of the first killed. His father was right, it had been his brother's place to go. John would have known how to fight.

Thomas knew he thought about things too much, but he vowed to try to learn to fight better. He looked around. After all, these men arrayed across the grass were exactly the right people to teach him. He firmed his shoulders and stepped toward one group that looked a little less fearsome than the others to ask if they could show him how to stay alive in the heat of battle.

THE THOMAS BERRINGTON HISTORICAL MYSTERIES

The Red Hill

Moorish Spain, 1482. English surgeon Thomas Berrington is asked to investigate a series of brutal murders in the palace of al-Hamra in Granada.

Breaker of Bones

Summoned to Cordoba to heal a Spanish prince, Thomas Berrington and his companion, the eunuch Jorge, pursue a killer who re-makes his victims with his own crazed logic.

The Sin Eater

In Granada Helena, the concubine who once shared Thomas Berrington's bed, is carrying his child, while Thomas tracks a killer exacting revenge on evil men.

The Incubus

A mysterious killer stalks the alleys of Ronda. Thomas Berrington, Jorge and Lubna race to identify the culprit before more victims have their breath stolen.

The Inquisitor

In a Sevilla on the edge of chaos death stalks the streets. Thomas Berrington and his companions tread a dangerous path between the Inquisition, the royal palace, and a killer.

The Fortunate Dead

As a Spanish army gathers outside the walls of Malaga, Thomas Berrington hunts down a killer who threatens more than just strangers.

The Promise of Pain

When revenge is not enough. Thomas Berrington flees to the high mountains, only to be drawn back by those he left behind.

The Message of Blood

When Thomas Berrington is sent to Cordoba on the orders of a man he hates he welcomes the distraction of a murder, but is shocked when the evidence points to the killer being his closest companion.

ABOUT THE AUTHOR

David Penny is the author of the Thomas Berrington Historical Mysteries set in Moorish Spain at the end of the 15th Century. He is currently working on the next book in the series.

Find out more about David Penny
www.davidpenny.com